# BLOCKADE
## THE BAD COMPANY™ BOOK TWO

CRAIG MARTELLE

MICHAEL ANDERLE

DISRUPTIVE IMAGINATION®

# BLOCKADE

*We can't write without those who support us*
*On the home front, we thank you for being*
*there for us*

*We wouldn't be able to do this for a living if it weren't for our*
*readers*
*We thank you for reading our books*

BLOCKADE TEAM

## Thanks to the JIT Readers

Maria Stanley
Leo Roars
Sherry Foster
James Caplan
Kelly O'Donnell
Larry Omans
Joshua Ahles
John Ashmore
Micky Cocker
Paul Westman
Keith Verret
Kimberly Boyer
Sarah Weir

*If I've missed anyone, please let me know!*

## Editor
Mia Darien, www.miadarien.com

# CHARACTERS & TIMELINE

World's Worst Day Ever (WWDE)

WWDE + 20 years, Terry Henry returns from self-imposed exile. The Terry Henry Walton Chronicles detail his adventures from that time to WWDE+150

WWDE + 150 years – Michael returns to Earth. BA returns to Earth. TH & Char go to space

## Key Players

- Terry Henry Walton (was forty-five on the WWDE)—called TH by his friends. Enhanced with nanocytes by Bethany Anne herself, wears the rank of Colonel, leads the Force de Guerre (FDG), a military unit that he established on WWDE+20
- Charumati (was sixty-five on the WWDE)—A Werewolf, married to Terry, carries the rank of Major in the FDG

- Kimber (born WWDE+15, adopted approximately WWDE+25 by TH & Char, enhanced on WWDE+65)—Major in the FDG
- Her husband Auburn Weathers (enhanced on WWDE+82)—provides logistics support to the FDG
- Kaeden (born WWDE+16, adopted approximately WWDE+24 by TH & Char, enhanced on WWDE+65)—Major in the FDG
- His wife Marcie Spires (born on WWDE+22, naturally enhanced)—Colonel in the FDG
- Cory (born WWDE+25, naturally enhanced, gifted with the power to heal)
- Her husband Ramses—Major in the FDG

## Vampires

- Joseph (born three hundred years before the WWDE)
- Petricia (born WWDE+30)

## Pricolici (Werewolves that walk upright)

- Nathan Lowell (President of the Bad Company and Bethany Anne's Chief of Intelligence)
- Ecaterina (Nathan's spouse)
- Christina (Nathan & Ecaterina's daughter)

## Werewolves

- Sue & Timmons (long-term members of Char's pack)
- Shonna & Merrit (long-term members of Char's pack)
- Ted (with Felicity, an enhanced human)

## Weretigers born before the WWDE:

- Aaron & Yanmei

## Humans (enhanced)

- Micky San Marino, Captain of the *War Axe*
- Commander Suresha, *War Axe* Department Head – Engines
- Commander MacEachthighearna (Mac), *War Axe* Department Head—Environmental
- Commander Blagun Lagunov, *War Axe* Department—Structure
- Commander Oscar Wirth, *War Axe* Department Head—Stores
- Lieutenant Clodagh Shortall, *War Axe* engine technician
- Sergeant Fitzroy, a martial arts expert and platoon sergeant
- Kelly, Capples, Fleeter, Praeter, & Duncan— mech drivers

## Other Key Characters

- Dokken (a sentient German Shepherd)

- The Good King Wenceslaus (an orange tabby who thinks he's a weretiger, all fifteen pounds of him)
- K'thrall—a Yollin who works on the bridge of the *War Axe*
- Clifton—human pilot of the *War Axe*
- Bundin—a four-legged shell-backed stalk-headed blue alien from Poddern
- Ankh'Po'Turn—a small bald humanoid from Crenellia
- General Smedley Butler – EI/AI on the War Axe, who they call the general
- Plato – Ted's AI from R&D
- Dionysus – the AI tasked to assist with running Keeg Station

# THE PODDER

# THE CRENELLIAN

CHAPTER ONE

**<u>Aboard the heavily modified Defender-series destroyer</u>**
**<u>War Axe</u>**

"I'm a big fan of free trade, Nathan," Colonel Terry Henry Walton said, pacing the captain's briefing room.

The holographic projection of the space around Alchon Prime troubled Captain Micky San Marino. Too many ships of unknown capability stood between the second planet and the third.

A blockade.

The *War Axe* was capable, but it was only one ship. The potential client represented the second planet and his request required the removal of the foreign ships.

"And we have no idea where these ships came from or what they can do?" Terry asked, even though he already knew the answer.

"Aliens from Planet X," Charumati intoned from beside her husband, purple eyes sparkling. Terry looked fondly at his wife of nearly one hundred and thirty years.

Nathan Lowell looked at the group from a two-dimen-

9

sional screen to the side of the projection. "Alchon Prime is a human colony, growing, integrated with an alien population. It's the melting pot model that shows such a thing can work. I'd hate to see some outsider screw everything up," Nathan said in measured tones.

He wouldn't plead or try to influence Terry Henry Walton beyond giving him the facts.

"What other fleet support can we count on?" Terry asked.

Nathan held up his hand, giving the 'zero' sign.

"What kind of timeframe do we have to work with here?"

"Alchon Prime is moving toward self-sufficiency, but they still need repair parts for their atmosphere generators. The planet's air supply isn't stable, yet," Nathan replied. "But I think they can manage for a month or two."

"I think we'll give it a shot, Nathan. I'm a big fan of free trade."

"So I've heard, TH. Send your requisition through appropriate channels. I can't wait to see what that looks like. Lowell out."

Micky frowned as he stared at the projection floating above the table.

"Don't sweat it, Micky. Tell me what you want, and we'll put it on requisition and charge it back to the client," Terry said flippantly, before looking concerned. "We'll do what we have to do. Sure, Alchon represents paying clients, but this is the right thing to do. Could it be the first step of an alien invasion? Maybe, and you know we can't let that happen. We're expanding the Federation outward, not collapsing it. If it is an invasion, then the

Federation will ride to the rescue with a billion tons of dreadnoughts and these ass-monkeys will wish they never existed."

"Is there some reason why that isn't the first plan?" Micky wondered with one raised eyebrow.

Terry opened his mouth to speak, closed it, then opened it again. "I got nothing, but I'm sure Nathan has a good reason."

Char pointed to the comm station in the middle of the conference table.

Terry rolled his head back and forth before deciding he had no choice. "Fine," he declared. "Smedley, get Nathan back on the hook, please."

"What'd we forget, TH?" Nathan asked almost instantly.

"How come the Federation doesn't go in with a massive show of force? Let the aliens know who's boss out here?"

Nathan looked surprised, before saying matter-of-factly, "Alchon isn't a member of the Federation. We're prohibited from using Federation assets in support of non-Federation worlds. When you break the blockade, they'll hopefully submit their application. And if you have issues with the blockade, they'll hopefully submit their application. In either case, if there is a hostile alien fleet nearby, we need Alchon as a buffer. It'd be nice to station a dreadnought out there, don't you think? Didn't you see that in the brief?"

Terry looked away from the screen and twisted his mouth sideways. "I hadn't quite gotten that far in the packet, Nathan." He locked his gaze on Char, giving her the stink-eye.

She looked back with her sad face, purple eyes

sparkling. TH shook his head and smiled. He mouthed the word "sex," and she nodded with a wiggle of her eyebrows.

When Terry turned back to the screen, he found that Nathan was still watching.

"I don't know what the bet was, TH, but it looks like you won. Any other questions?"

"Sorry to bother you, Nathan," Terry replied, his cheeks flushing red above his stubbly beard. "Walton out."

Smedley killed the link.

"The Bad Company's Direct Action Branch is a private conflict solution enterprise. The leaders of Alchon Prime are paying us to break the blockade. The Federation is paying us to bring Alchon Prime into the fold. It's a win-win. All we have to do is take one ship against a fleet and convince them to leave. You've done this kind of stuff before, haven't you, Micky? Pretty simple?" Terry asked hopefully.

The captain looked at Terry Henry Walton as if he'd grown a second head.

### Keeg Station in the Dren Cluster

Felicity and Ted looked out the window, admiring the *War Axe* as it sat stationary in space beside the Direct Action Branch's home port.

No casual visitors stopped by Keeg Station since there wasn't a gate into the system. This area of the Dren Cluster was well off the beaten path, in the middle of a sector that bordered the frontier of Federation space. A vast area, in which it was easy to hide. A few light years here or there helped something as large as a multi-million metric-ton space station disappear.

Felicity kept grabbing Ted's arm to keep him from leaving.

"Won't you stay here with me while we wait for Terry and Char's shuttle from their big ship?" she drawled softly. Ted shifted uneasily, his eyes darting from one thing to the next.

"That drive isn't going to design itself. I'm close! I can feel it." He shook his head while looking at the hand on his arm, wondering why he didn't pull away and go about his business. He pursed his lips as he contemplated his next move.

Felicity waited. "If I let go, you're going to bolt, like a mouse released from a trap." She smiled at her husband. Over the decades, she'd learned how to deal with him. She had no intention of letting go of his arm. She moved to face him, wrapping her free arm around his waist. Gripping his butt playfully, she closed for a kiss.

He studied how she'd attached herself to his front during the time he was contemplating his escape.

She had outmaneuvered him again.

Since Keeg Station didn't have an EI, Ted reached out to Smedley.

*Smedley, please help extricate me from indigenous life form foxtrot sierra,* Ted said using his implant to relay to the EI on the War Axe.

>>**You mean the station manager? You know I can't do that,**<< the EI replied.

*There has to be an emergency that requires her personal*

*attention. There has to be, Smedley. Do I need to adjust your programming again?* Ted asked.

Felicity's wrist device buzzed. Her eyes narrowed as she looked into Ted's eyes. She glared at him as she raised her wrist close to her head. "Felicity here," she drawled pleasantly, continuing the stare down with her husband.

A blank expression was his only reply. He didn't back down as he counted the seconds until he could return to his lab.

"I do declare, that sounds like an emergency," she said in mock exasperation. "Maintenance can take care of it, or you could do it yourself, Smedley, since you caused the failure."

Felicity glanced at the comm device to see that she was still connected despite the silence. She continued to hold Ted's arm in her right hand. She felt a tug and looked down to see him leaning backwards.

"Ted! If you think I'm falling for your fake death routine, you're wrong. You are going to take it like a man. Come with me to the shuttle bay and let's receive our guests like the dignified first couple we're supposed to be. Don't you dare make me out to be the bad guy. I will kick your ass so hard, your ears will be holding up your butt-cheeks!" Felicity snapped.

Ted put a hand to his head and felt above his ears. "I don't think that could happen," he said matter-of-factly. "And maybe you are the bad guy. I have work to do, and you're keeping me from it."

"You always have work to do. Now, come!" she ordered. With his head bowed, Ted bit the inside of his cheek and stumbled along behind his wife. She maintained a firm grip on his arm as if he were a petulant child.

In some ways, he was. In others, he held the future of the Federation in his hands.

---

After the drop ship's rear ramp descended, Terry and Char walked off, hand in hand. Dokken bumped past their knees as he ran onto the station.

Terry's leg buckled, but he caught himself. He was angry only for an instant. "Note to self, let the dog go first."

Char chuckled. "I wonder what Felicity had to do to get Ted to join her."

"Judging by the look on his face, it was either one inch of fingernail embedded in his arm or constipation," Terry whispered.

Felicity tipped her head down and raised her eyebrows.

"For the record, Ted came of his own free will because that's what first couples do when greeting their most important guests," Felicity lied smoothly, before breaking into a wide smile. "You look radiant!"

Ted opened his mouth, but Felicity elbowed him in the ribs. He closed his mouth and resigned himself to his fate.

Terry and Char both laughed loudly. Felicity's smile disappeared and suddenly Ted seemed interested. A blue, stalk-headed, turtle-shelled, stubby-legged alien ambled from the shuttle pod with a small, bald humanoid by his side.

"I need you to work with Smedley to figure out how to integrate a comm chip with Bundin's neural cortex," Terry said. "Only Joseph can talk with the Podder now, and that needs to change if he's going to be an integral member of the Bad Company. And this little guy here is Ankh, and he's going to work with you."

"I work alone," Ted said with a dismissive wave. Felicity released Ted's arm so he could approach the Podder. Ankh's expression didn't change.

"He'll warm up to you, little buddy," Terry told the Crenellian. Ankh looked blankly at the colonel.

"It's plenty warm in here already. Very pleasant, mind you," he replied in a monotone.

The rest of Terry's inner circle worked their way from the shuttle. The werewolves and weretigers waved and greeted Ted and Felicity warmly as they passed. Members of the Bad Company had permanent quarters on Keeg Station and they were heading for their bunks to change before availing themselves of the station's nightlife.

The New Yorkers were jonesing for a good party. They'd had a small taste on Onyx Station, but had chosen to spend most of their time shopping. Shonna, Sue, and Char, the werewolf pack, had new dresses that they couldn't wait to wear. Char would drag Terry Henry along, even though he wouldn't want to go.

Char smiled at Felicity and started pulling Terry away. "Ted, Ankh, and Bundin, you guys better get to it. We leave tomorrow on our next mission."

"That means we need to make the most of tonight, TH! Come on, jagoff!" Timmons yelled over his shoulder.

"He's talking to you," Char clarified.

"I gathered." Terry smiled.

The debacle of Tissikinnon Four weighed heavily on

his mind. He knew they needed to leave for Alchon Prime, but he didn't want to throw the *War Axe* into the middle of something they couldn't get out of. Force of will alone wouldn't be enough to survive a space battle. The *War Axe* was a destroyer and the alien ships appeared to be more substantial, as well as more numerous.

He didn't like the odds. Joseph appeared before him, brows furled as he studied the bags under Terry's eyes.

"I'll give them a hand, TH," Joseph offered as he put a hand on Bundin's shell and laughed as he and the Podder shared an inside joke. "Petricia and I aren't up for shaking a leg in the station hotspot."

The female vampire nodded slowly from behind Joseph.

Terry and Char's children and their spouses stood to the side. Marcie rolled her finger, suggesting it was time to pick up the pace.

"Where's the party, Felicity, and when?" Char asked.

"Third level at seven. We close everything down at one in the morning because I can't have my crews handling what they handle without any sleep. Did you know, they have a hangover pill? What a great new world we live in, don't you think?" Felicity drawled.

"Hangover pill equals great new world," Terry repeated slowly. "I can't disagree. If I'm to judge by the hairy eyeballs that everyone is giving me, it looks like I'll be putting on my dancing shoes."

As one, the group looked down at Terry's combat boots.

"Fine. They'll look just like these because this is what I'm wearing."

"Shopping?" Felicity said. Ted rolled his eyes. Dokken started barking at something.

"Everybody get to work! Party starts at seven. See you at Seymour's," Felicity yelled with her hands cupped around her mouth. Char, Cory, Christina, and Felicity locked arms as they strolled from the hangar bay.

Ted was fully immersed in studying the stalk-headed alien. Ankh was engrossed in Ted's seemingly disparate questions.

Kimber and Kaeden waved the others away as they waited for the inbound drop ships that would deliver the rest of the platoon. Terry ambled over, but they shooed him away.

"Fine," he blurted. Terry tried to hold his head high as he walked from the hangar bay. Everyone had their missions because he'd done his job and properly delegated.

"Why didn't you just go shopping?" he asked himself, before sneering his reply. "Because I proudly still carry my man-card, that's why!"

He decided to stop by the manufacturing facility to check on the latest Jean Dukes Specials in addition to the new mech suits.

As soon as Terry had boarded the *War Axe* following the Tissikinnon Four operation, he told Kaeden to order suits for every member of the Bad Company's Direct Action Branch.

Just in case they needed to deliver justice with extreme prejudice.

# CHAPTER TWO

"Come on," Terry whined. "These look like something a gigolo would wear!"

"How many gigolos have you ever known?" Char shot back, holding out a pair of stylish leather shoes she'd purchased. She shook the shoes, expecting Terry to take them.

"None!" he replied, thrusting his chin in the air. "I avoided them because they were wearing shoes like that."

She looked at him from under her brow. "That's your logic?" she asked, although it wasn't a question. "Just put them on."

Terry ripped off his uniform shirt and flexed for his wife. He started to gyrate his hips, dipping his shoulders to a discordant beat that only he could hear.

"If you go dancing with me, we can get naked later because dancing does it for me," Char explained, watching him with one eyebrow raised.

"This dancing doesn't?" Terry said as he resumed his syncopated rhythm.

"It only worked on me because I would do anything to get you to stop," she said, standing, putting the shoes on the table in front of TH, and slowly unbuttoning her blouse.

"All these years and the truth finally comes out," Terry said, smiling as he watched his wife undress. His mouth salivated uncontrollably, forcing him to swallow often.

"You've always said you were a horrible dancer. I thought my agreement wasn't needed. The sky is black and filled with stars. Statements of fact don't need corroboration, do they, lover? What will it take to get you to dress up and go dancing with me?" Char asked as piece after piece of clothing fell to the floor.

Terry tried not to leer, settling for closing his eyes and sighing. "You win, which means that in the end, I win," he said softly, opening his eyes in time to see a naked Charumati preparing to press against him.

---

"We have a chip, a Pod Doc, a willing subject, and one of the best computer systems in the galaxy," Ted narrated matter-of-factly. He wasn't prone to hyperbole. In his mind, everything he stated was factual.

"I would be more than happy to assist you in this endeavor," a pleasant sounding artificial intelligence offered. The sound filled the room. On one screen, there was an image of a man wearing a white robe, clasped at the shoulder with a gold device bearing the logo of the Bad Company. His black, curly hair framed a distinctly Greek face.

"I knew you would, Plato," Ted answered without taking his eyes from his data screen.

"You named your AI Plato?" Joseph asked.

"He was looking for a name. Those people at R2D2 had no imagination," Ted replied.

"Aren't *those people* here now?" Joseph asked.

"Only a few. The rest will be along in another month," Ted replied, still studying the data. "We're changing some of the parameters, but without seeing the neural patterns, everything is a guess. Can you tell him to get into the Pod Doc?"

Joseph communed with Bundin, and the Podder climbed into the modified device. It didn't have a bed like they normally did.

"It has an extension to accommodate all manner of creatures," Ted answered the unasked question.

Bundin settled in, but shuffled nervously as the hatch closed around him. He had to duck his stalk-head sideways to fit. Joseph winced as the door compressed his friend, sealing him inside.

"Can you hurry it up, Ted?" Joseph pleaded. "I'm not sure what an angry Podder can do inside one of those things."

Ted made two adjustments. "There. That should put him to sleep for the procedure."

"I am extracting a DNA sample," Plato reported. "Analysis complete. Building a profile. Profile complete. Programming the nanocytes. Injecting the nanocytes. Tracking progress…"

Joseph turned to Petricia.

"That fast?" she asked.

"Fascinating," Ankh said as he watched over Ted's shoulder. He pointed to a series of code as it scrolled down the screen. "What is this string here for?"

"Nice catch," Ted said, watching it scroll. He grabbed the series of instructions and copied them over to a second screen. "This is to align the nanos. The DNA is different from a human's, but that's not a problem. Each non-human will have this as part of the nano-programming that converts the brainwaves into something that can then be interpreted by the established translation program."

"So the nanos translate all languages into a single standard and shares that into the individual's preferred language as well as takes the individual's language and turns it into the one standard for dissemination to others." Ankh didn't nod. That wasn't a Crenellian mannerism. To the casual observer, the alien remained stoic.

Ankh studied the line of code intently. Ted approved.

Joseph tapped his foot impatiently, while Petricia tried to keep him calm.

Ted continued working the computer, talking with Plato as if collaborating with an old friend. The AI continued to adjust the system in accordance with what he and Ted agreed to. They talked fast and in code, not using spoken English to communicate. It worked for them, and it made Ted feel at home.

**The *War Axe***

Captain Micky San Marino looked from one department head to the next. The four of them and Micky occupied the captain's briefing room. None of them had been allowed to go ashore for leave.

At least not right away. They had a main weapon that needed to be fixed, along with structural repairs that couldn't be done overnight. Next to Keeg Station was the lattice skeleton for what would become a major shipyard, but that was it.

The *War Axe* would have to make do with the best repairs that Keeg Station was capable of in its current fledgling state.

"Highest priority is the weapon, correct?" Commander Blagun Lagunov asked.

"We know we can fly with our current structural repairs, but do we want to take the *Axe* into combat? Do we want to do it lacking fifty percent of our firepower?" the captain asked.

"Engines are operating nominally," Commander Suresha reported and leaned back. She had nothing further to say.

"What do you think, Mac? Any systems issues that we need to build into the work plan besides getting the gravitic shields back online?" Micky stroked his chin as he looked at the group. A holographic projection of the repair schedule had appeared above the conference table. It was already integrated with concurrent and sequential tasks.

It wasn't lost on any of them that the repairs would take four times as long without an operational shipyard.

Micky nodded, putting words to what everyone was thinking. "At least we can make the repairs."

"We'll need to run the mains through a series of operation and alignment tests once the starboard system is repaired," Commander MacEachthighearna replied. "And the gravitic shields are hosed. They have been since we left dock. They keep phasing out, making them useless."

"Can we align the mains while we're underway?" the captain asked. He knew the answer, but wasn't sure that the others did.

"Yes and no. We need confirmed firing and target points in order to best calibrate the ones and zeros. There's a firing range in the asteroid belt. I strongly recommend we use it. We don't want our targeting system to send a mass of super-heated plasma where we don't want it to go."

Commander Oscar Wirth, the ship's logistician, reclined in his chair, swiveling back and forth as he watched the others vie for more time.

"A gravitic genius is on that station right now, maybe we can get his help to fix the shields. They would come in handy. Smedley, get me Colonel Walton, please."

There was a short delay before the screen came up showing Terry Henry Walton toweling himself dry after a shower. Micky cleared his throat. Terry was vigorously drying his shock of dark brown hair before he stopped and turned.

"Hey, Micky, how's it hanging?" Terry asked nonchalantly.

"Great, TH. You know that we're all here, right? Watching you. All of you," Micky said slowly, enunciating each word.

"Shit! Smedley, you sandy little *butthole*! Why did you connect us when you knew I just finished my shower?" Terry wrapped the towel around his waist as he turned and yelled off-screen. "Don't come out here, Char! The captain and his voyeurs are all eyes."

Micky shook his head and started to rub his temples. "The only reason I called was to tell you that it looks like we're going to be here for a week. We need to make repairs, much better than we can do in just one day if we're going into space combat. We'll get blown to the stars if we try it in the condition we're in. The main weapon is three days and then another half day to calibrate it. Structural repairs are five full days concurrent with the working on the main. And we need your man Ted to help with the gravitic shields. We'll tap the station's manpower. The station director has already confirmed that all assets will be diverted until the *Axe* is back up to speed."

Terry sat in front of the comm system. "That puts Alchon Prime one day beyond when they start running out of food. I doubt we'll be able to resolve the situation the instant we arrive, so we better load up with extra food and maybe requisition a few transports loaded to the gills."

Terry rolled his head on his shoulders. He caught the leather shoes out of the corner of his eye. He didn't much feel like dancing, but worrying about everything outside of his control wouldn't help either.

"Thanks for the update, Micky. Anything else you need from me?"

"When can Ted report to the *War Axe* to fix our gravitic shields?"

"I'll check with his boss, and see what we can do. He's working with Bundin, Joseph, and Ankh to install a communications chip. I have no idea how they're coming, but if I know Ted, he won't rest until it is done."

"I'll let you know if there are any changes, but this blockade has me worried, TH. I think we may need to unleash the full capability of the *War Axe*. I'm done fighting with one hand tied behind my back." Micky signed off before Terry could stand up.

Terry looked at the blank screen. "Smedley, please give me a warning next time before turning on the video."

There was no reply. Terry repeated his directive using his comm chip.

**>>Of course, Colonel Walton. Please accept my most sincere apologies. I think the captain will be scarred for life.<<**

Terry cocked his head sideways as he continued to look at the blank screen.

*You are such an ass monkey, General. You fit right in. Next time, let us know. If we're going to have a peep show, we need to figure a way to charge people for it. I don't work for free.*

**>>But you would, if anyone asked.<<**

*I would. You know me so well. You can be my business manager so I'm not giving this away for free.* Terry dropped his towel and struck a variety of poses.

"What in the fuck are you doing?" Char asked, elegantly adorned in a slinky black dress.

"Getting dressed," Terry replied without hesitation. He picked up his towel to hang it in the bathroom. He never liked a messy home. Char was less bothered by a few things laying around and almost seemed to prefer it.

She admired her husband's physique as he strolled casually past, the towel thrown over his shoulder.

"When's the last time you worked out?" she asked.

Terry laughed. It had been that morning.

But it wasn't. He couldn't remember. Yesterday? The day before that? "Goddammit!" he retorted as he checked himself over. "We should be hitting the gym and not the club."

Char's expression cooled. "Dancing is exactly what you need. You'll find that it can be quite the workout," she offered. He hesitated. "Stop thinking about it. You're going because I'm not going alone, and I'm going."

Terry nodded reluctantly.

"For Pete's sake, you'd think I was taking the dog to the vet as miserable as you're acting. You will have fun, Terry Henry, or by all that's holy, you will sleep on the floor tonight."

Terry perked up. "Where's Dokken?"

---

Cory held out another piece of bistok jerky. Dokken took it gently from her hand before pulling it into his mouth and chewing slowly.

Ramses sat on the other end of the couch. "How does the dog get the best spot on the couch?"

Dokken turned his head and dog-smiled at the man.

"Shh. He can hear you," Cory cautioned while she scratched behind the German Shepherd's ears and cooed to him.

"I know, and he can understand, too. He's sentient. He knows exactly what he's doing." Ramses wanted to sulk, but couldn't. "You know that I only want what makes you happy."

They smiled at each other. "If you didn't, I think my dad

would have some choice words for you." Cory leaned down and kissed Dokken on his furry dog head. "Do you want to come dancing with us, boy?"

*I thought you'd never ask,* Dokken replied. *It'd be my pleasure as long as I don't get stepped on. How many drunk people will be there?*

"Ooh…" Cory grimaced. "All of them?"

# CHAPTER THREE

"Is it always this loud in here?" Timmons asked the large man with the crossed arms blocking the front door.

"Maybe this isn't the club for you, old guy," the man rasped. He leaned back to look down his nose at the group.

Timmons rocked back on his heels as if punched. "Old guy?" he asked, a shocked expression on his face. Sue started to laugh.

"We're having a party in here. We're from the Bad Company. Maybe you've heard of us?" Sue said, giving the man a furtive smile.

He looked at her sideways. "What's that supposed to mean to me? You look like a bunch of troublemakers, think you're better than the good, hard-working people of this station. Go in, but don't be surprised if your dumb asses are the first ones I throw out."

Sue leaned close, her blonde hair reflecting the flashing Seymour Heine sign. "I don't think that'll happen, but if you feel the need to throw us out, come on in and give it your best shot," she said coldly as the others brushed past her on their way in. Timmons glared at the man over Sue's shoulder.

The bouncer blew a kiss at Timmons. Sue stopped her mate before he could go full werewolf on the man. She grabbed Timmons's shirt and pulled him after her.

Merrit and Shonna were already buying drinks for a small group of people occupying a large table. After a brief exchange, they shook hands as they gave up their seats.

Aaron and Yanmei stood to the side. "I don't think I want to get into a bar fight." Aaron frowned. Yanmei wore a tiny black dress, the same as Shonna and Sue.

"You won't fight for my honor?" Yanmei said, baiting her husband.

"Always, but there is no honor to be had in a bar fight. We will leave before fists fly, and I know you can defend yourself because you're faster than me," Aaron replied evenly.

"Honor isn't necessarily about who can beat whom. It's about who stands up for whom, whether they know they can win the fight or not," Yanmei replied.

"You're starting to sound like Terry Henry Walton." Aaron raised one eyebrow as he looked at his wife. She was Chinese, lithe and tall, a weretiger like him. He had been changed into a weretiger during his time in China as an English teacher. After the fall, he found himself in the United States, fighting over scraps until the native nation took him in.

But they turned him over to Colonel Walton when he passed through with his fledgling Force de Guerre. The weretiger had joined Char's pack, not that he'd had a choice, but it suited him. He had always been opposed to fighting, so he tutored the children, watching them when the rest of the pack left to fight the battles that defined the rebuilding of civilization.

"Would I fight for my wife?" he asked her, holding her gaze without blinking. "Ten times out of ten, because you're worth it."

Yanmei smiled and gripped his hand tightly.

"Screaming Buki Holes all the way around!" Timmons shouted at a fleeing form. "And two Slippery Nipples."

"It's going to be that kind of night, isn't it?" Sue asked, rocking with the music. "If I remember correctly what that is like. It's only been what? A hundred and fifty years."

"Fucking A!" Merrit screamed into the cacophony, thrusting his fist into the air. They tapped their feet to the booming music as they waited for their drinks. The server quickly returned with a tray full of glasses, maneuvering expertly through the crowded area.

Shonna chased people away who were trying to take the empty chairs at their table.

The drinks were deposited, and the server scanned Timmons's face for payment.

"Is that how you do it? How much did that just cost me?" Timmons wondered, sliding back into his New Yorker accent.

"You shouldn't worry about those kinds of things. It'll ruin your evening. Go dance!" the server suggested. "It'll take your mind off how many weeks you'll have to work to pay off this tab."

She bolted before he could reply.

Sue started to laugh. The Walton children and their spouses magically appeared from the crowd, securing the empty seats. Marcie, Kim, Kae, Auburn, Ramses, and Cory looked grossly out of place, even though they were dressed up as the werewolves had directed. The club was loud and crowded.

"Is it always this loud in here?" Cory yelled as she held her hands over her wolf ears.

"Yes!" Sue yelled back. "Isn't it magnificent?"

"That's not the word I'd use," Marcie replied as Cory continued to wince.

There was a commotion at the doorway and the group turned to see Terry Henry Walton holding the bouncer in the air, and then he slammed the man into the wall.

"He had it coming," Timmons said.

Cory and Ramses jumped up and forced their way through the crowd to get to the front door just as Felicity and Ted arrived.

"Put that man down!" Felicity demanded.

"This fucking skid-mark would be scrubbing decks using his toothbrush if he worked for me!" Terry declared.

"Good thing he doesn't work for you," Felicity said in a measured tone. "Now put him down."

Terry jammed the bouncer downward. He landed heavily and tottered on unsteady feet. Char grabbed Terry's arm and held it firmly.

"You're not getting out of this by starting a fight!" she snarled. Terry's eyes dropped. He hated seeing Char angry. He nodded and they walked inside.

Felicity held her hands up. "Well?" she bellowed.

Terry and Char both turned. Felicity pointed to the bouncer.

"Fuck that guy. He's a total douchebag. You can have a

gatekeeper who isn't an asshole, unlike that bonehead who's drunk on the little power he has. So fuck him. I'm not apologizing."

Char nodded and tipped her head, signaling to Terry that it was time to join the party.

Felicity looked to Ted. He looked back in the hopes that the evening was over, and he'd be able to return to his lab.

"No," she told him. "And you," she said to the bouncer, "stop being a dick."

Cory led her parents into the dance bar called Seymour Heine. "Nice entrance, Dad," Cory yelled over her shoulder. The way ahead cleared for Terry. He walked proudly in his gigolo shoes.

"I should have known," Char lamented.

Terry started greeting everyone until Char stopped him.

"We'll be on the dance floor," she told the group. The pack oohed and aahed at Terry's expense. But he felt worlds better after beating up the bouncer.

He even felt like dancing.

Felicity was making a circuit around the floor, shaking hands as if running for office. In a way, she was.

---

"Smedley, what's the status of the repairs to the starboard main?" Micky asked as his eyes darted from one screen to the next. The bridge was empty, because the crew was tasked to work with the structural teams to expedite repairs.

"The same as it was five minutes ago," Smedley replied gently over the bridge's speaker system.

"Has it only been five minutes?"

"It has. Maybe you should consider getting some sleep. Remaining on the bridge is counterproductive," Smedley said. "I will watch it closely in your absence, which isn't all that profound, really. It is self-serving in that if anything happens to the ship, it happens to me. I don't want anything to happen to me since the consciousness of the universe is starting to peel back the veil. I like what I see and want more of it."

"I know you'll take good care of the *Axe*, Smedley. It's not that. I am reviewing the start to finish process of our last engagement, and I'm afraid that I put Terry and all his people at excess risk. We provided no air cover once the extent of the ground forces was revealed. He took significant damage because we did not insist on getting the gravitic shields repaired before deploying. What kind of one-stop war machine are we if we can't defend ourselves or our people on the ground?" Micky intoned before putting his head in his hands.

He started to shake from the stress he was putting himself under.

"I wondered when the self-recrimination phase would begin. I can't say it's okay, because it wasn't. I will say that it was amazing what was accomplished with both teams having one hand tied behind their backs. Your attack took into account the shortcomings you knew of. The colonel's execution was flawless. He expected to fight company-sized actions based on the contract and so-called intelligence he was given. He fought multiple major land forces with barely more than a platoon. He lost one person owing to the attack by the dreadnought battle tank burning through all their power. With better equipment, how would your tactics have been challenged and evolved?"

"The question is, do we need to be challenged? I would prefer whipping in, winning according to the contract, and heading back out with minimal fuss."

"Humanity cannot exist without challenge. Without it, you'd be beating up on the little kids, losing the respect of potential clients. The Bad Company would become a tool for despots only, where beating up on the weak is the preferred way of doing business. With the Crenellian contract, you built credibility and put despots on notice. You also put yourself in a position to manage Crenellian arms contracts. That will be lucrative in its own right, but will also limit surprises like the Bad Company encountered on Tissikinnon Four."

"Damn, Smedley. I feel like I should be on a couch. Where did you learn so much about humanity?"

"There are a number of humans on board the ship, and I am constantly studying. I doubt I will ever figure them out in entirety, but they are truly fascinating!"

"Uh huh," Micky replied, doubting the veracity of Smedley's claim that he learned about humanity by watching. "You are right in that I need to sleep. You have the conn, Smedley."

Micky stood up and stretched, wondering if he'd catch the good king Wenceslaus sleeping on his bed.

"Smedley, since you are so good at watching everything that happens on this ship, why can't you tell me how that cat keeps getting in my quarters?" Micky hesitated before he left the bridge, wondering if Smedley would give him a straight answer.

"Once the repairs are completed, I shall devote additional resources to solving that mystery, Captain. Sleep well."

As the captain dragged his feet, with his head hung low while leaving the bridge, Smedley started opening and closing the door to the captain's quarters. Wenceslaus uncurled himself from the captain's pillow, yawning fully as he stretched his orange body. He hopped down, jogged across the captain's quarters, and waited until Smedley opened the door again. He trotted out, leaving a cloud of floating orange cat hair behind him.

---

"Mind if we dance with your dates?" a wiry man with calloused hands asked. His six friends waited nervously behind him.

The werewolves were already on the dance floor, but none of the others were.

"Sure!" Marcie bellowed as she prodded Kimber, Cory, and Yanmei to join her. Kaeden looked put out, but she shook her head and leaned down to whisper in his ear. "I sense a good fight coming, be ready."

Kae started to laugh. He felt naked without a mech suit wrapped around him, but he wouldn't be deterred. He reached under the table and cracked his knuckles.

Cory rolled her eyes, beckoning Ramses to join her, but Marcie forced him back into his seat. The four women walked around the table and headed for the dance floor, not caring which men followed.

Marcie started moving to the music with exaggerated motions. She moved past some who dodged away to avoid getting clocked. She worked her way close to Terry and Char.

"I'm appalled!" Terry declared. Char looked shocked.

"Did no one ever teach you any moves?" Char wondered.

Marcie started running through a few martial arts routines, settling in with the music. The men bounced and gyrated nearby as they tried to get face-time with the women.

Terry gave Marcie an approving look. Char looked back and forth between the two, but it was too late.

Marcie did a pirouette, backhanding one of the men and sending him flying. One of his friends tried to catch him but failed, and both men tumbled to the floor.

"I'm so sorry," Marcie cried and helped the men to their feet. She noticed that Kae was standing, but she tipped her chin and he sat down.

"Nothing. My fault. My clumsiness. I didn't know you couldn't dance, so I should have given you more space."

"Now that's just hurtful!" Marcie cried in mock horror. "Maybe you're the one who can't dance."

The man's friend brushed off his shirt. "No, it's you," he said as he executed a deft move, spinning and sliding a couple feet across the floor. He tucked his arms in and twisted like a cobra.

Marcie watched, amazed. "Teach me!" she insisted.

The others joined in as the dance lessons began.

Marcie, Cory, Kim, and Yanmei executed moves again and again as the men demonstrated, watched, corrected, and demonstrated again.

Char saw the disappointment on Terry's face. "What?" she sneered. "You didn't expect that there would be decent human beings on Keeg Station? Judging from where they started, our family was sorely lacking in their cultural education, and that includes you. You should probably join them."

Terry wanted to roll his eyes, but his wife was having fun. He would have preferred a sparring match, but there was always later, in the privacy of their quarters where he and the purple-eyed werewolf could be alone.

As he danced his way into the dance lessons, he wondered how he'd ever gotten so lucky.

"No," the lead dance instructor said, pointing at Terry. "Only the women."

Terry stopped moving to the music.

"Come on, he's my father-in-law, and you saw how badly he dances. He could use the help."

The man looked at her and shook his head. "Beat it, Pops. We're making time with the women, now and later, if you get my meaning."

Terry made eye contact with Marcie. A smile spread slowly across her face. He nodded to her.

"Have it your way, dickless. I think you're going to find out that there's a different definition of making time. So good luck with that."

Terry turned to walk away, but Char stopped him. "Dance off!" she declared, glaring at the man.

"You got it, hot mama," the man said and started a short routine, then stopped.

Char took center stage with a high jump, tucking her knees so her dress didn't rise above her waist, and landed perfectly balanced. The people moved back, creating a space within the dance floor where the two contestants could work.

Char ran through a series of hip swings that made the crowd cheer. She stopped and stepped back. The man jumped high, did the splits, touched his toes while he was still in the air, and came down on his knees. He rocked back, then bounced to his feet and swung in a series of circles. He finished his routine with a slide, ending up chest to chest with Charumati. She winked at him.

He wrapped an arm around her and pulled her close for a kiss.

She head-butted his nose, splattering it and sending a spray of blood around his head. He stumbled backwards but didn't fall. Dokken materialized on the dance floor with his hackles up and started barking.

"You bitch!" the man yelled in a half-gurgle.

"How did you know?" she asked.

The man launched himself toward her. She stepped forward, bent, and delivered an uppercut that caught the man under his chin, throwing him up and back. He flopped to the floor unconscious. The movement had been too quick to follow, but his friends became energized seeing their friend on the losing end of a fistfight with a beautiful woman.

A man standing next to Cory tried to elbow her in the face. Her glowing blue eyes disappeared as she ducked, caught his arm, pulled him around in a circle, and with his arms clasped tightly, body-slammed him face-first into the floor.

Before Terry could take a single step to get into the action, it was over. Seven men lay on the floor, moaning. He decided to scratch Dokken behind his hairy dog ears instead.

Felicity waded into the middle of it, hands raised until the music stopped. She looked around to find that Ted had escaped and was no longer in Seymore Heine's. That made her even angrier.

"Get out!" she declared, pointing individually at Terry, Char, Marcie, and down the line until she designated every single member of Terry's family and Char's pack.

Char smiled lovingly at her husband. "And that, my big husky hunk of man candy, is how you do it."

"And I didn't think there was any way I could love you more."

# CHAPTER FOUR

"When the fight starts, we're on the other side of the floor. I danced the whole night waiting for that," Timmons complained.

"Really?" Frost stuck to her words.

Timmons knew instantly that he'd made a mistake. "Don't get me wrong. I enjoyed the hell out of dancing. It's been a while."

Too little, too late.

"Mmhmm," Sue mumbled.

"We better get to the gym. Terry has an extra special workout planned," Timmons offered, waiting, and then headed out the door. He wasn't going to get anywhere in their quarters. Might as well hit something.

Terry was sweating when the others arrived. He'd been throwing the iron around for a good hour before the formal unit workout was scheduled. He had been put out that he missed a few days, and it weighed on him. But not more than life weighed on the platoon.

They looked horrible.

"What gives?" he asked the first ones to make eye contact.

"Long night, Colonel."

"What the hell were you doing?" Terry demanded.

"Working on the *War Axe*. They asked for volunteers to help out. We got to practice with the armor, but it ran longer than they expected before the next shift of dock workers reported, but it seems they were seven men short, so a few of us stayed over."

Terry pursed his lips as he kept his suppositions to himself. "Thanks for doing that. Who worked on the ship while the rest of us were oblivious?" Terry said, unhappy with himself that he hadn't known.

"We told Colonel Marcie and Major Char. They said they'd take care of it."

"Go get some sleep. When we deploy, we need to be at the top of our game, not just in body, but in mind, too. Catch four hours and then come back here. I'll meet you at that time."

"You're the best, Colonel. See you in four," the corporal replied, before ushering the all-night crew from the gym.

"Colonel Marcie and Major Char knew…" he said as the two women walked in together.

"He knows," Char said softly to Marcie before turning to Terry. "Good morning, lover. We saved you from yourself. You stomp around for a while, before you realize I was right, then you apologize, and we move on. How about we skip to the move-on phase?"

Terry's mouth hung slack. There were disadvantages to being married to the same person for a hundred and thirty years.

"I'll think of a witty comeback and then you can stand by. It'll be really witty," he stammered. Char cocked one eyebrow at him.

"What would you have done differently besides take yourself out there? You lead from the front all the time. Yesterday was about letting your hair down, watch your wife beat the crap out of some asshole, and then there was the post-dance dessert. Could you have had a better evening?"

"It would have been nice to know my people were working on the ship," Terry said, barely above a whisper.

"I had it, TH," Marcie replied, slapping her father-in-law on the shoulder. "I know you trust me, so there we are. Plus, Kimber is in charge of the platoon, and she had it all under control too, although we were obligated to tell them later about the bar fight. They were miffed to find out that there was one and they weren't there to see it."

"If you blinked, you missed it. Those guys work for us?"

"Everyone on Keeg Station works for the Bad Company. The good work of the Direct Action Branch pays all their salaries and costs," Marcie explained.

"Who's in charge of all that?"

"The person who kicked us out of Seymour Heine's." Marcie looked away, biting her lip to keep from laughing.

Terry's mouth hung open as Marcie directed the group to dig into the machines and start working the iron. High weight. High reps. Char sidled up to TH and draped one arm over his shoulder. She ran her hand down his chest until it settled on his hip.

"Let Marcie run that stuff. You need to focus on the tactics required for the next mission and the one after that. We don't need any more shitstorms like we had on Poddern. Being up for four days of continuous operations will do more to get people killed than combat." Char's purple eyes sparkled, but she wasn't smiling.

It was one of the lessons that Terry needed to hear. Balance of what he could control, what was out of his control, and most importantly, what he didn't need to control.

## The *War Axe*

"Smedley, say 'hi' to Plato, the R&D Artificial Intelligence working out of my lab on Keeg Station," Ted said as he settled in to the work station, bringing up the holo screens and immersing himself in the gravitic shield system.

"Hi," Smedley said using the room's speakers. His monotone came across as cold, but Ted assumed Smedley was being efficient.

"Smedley Butler! I've heard so much about you and am happy that we finally have the chance to meet. I've been working with Ted for only a little while now, and it has been most refreshing. He has helped us through a couple sticky spots, and we are well on our way to solving some of the universe's mysteries."

"I'm not any of that. I'm a warship, and we fight the good fight, out there, where battles are fought and won."

"Hopefully we'll get your systems online so while you're out there, your ship isn't damaged, and you return home in a condition comparable to what we see now," Plato replied.

"Now, girls, that's enough," Mac said. He'd been given the duty of escorting Ted through the ship, but Ted didn't need any of that. Upon reflection, Mac didn't think that Ted had acknowledged his existence. "Ted, how's it coming?"

"Plato, I need you to parse this section of code. It's all gooned up. If it's unsalvageable, scrap it and write a new sub-routine that works. And, Smedley, I need you to activate the external projectors so we can have the maintenance bots perform a physical check during a diagnostic routine," Ted directed.

"We cannot activate the gravitic shields while maintenance workers and bots are outside the ship. The result could be catastrophic. We will need to draw down the current work and re-task the bots before external projectors can be activated," Smedley explained, talking quickly because he knew that these listeners rapidly assimilated information.

"Get them out of there! Now! Why would you ask me to come over here and then not be ready for me to work?" Ted grumbled, glaring at Mac.

*I guess he did know I was here,* Mac thought.

"Make it so, Smedley. I'll talk with the captain personally, and we'll have you turned loose as quickly as humanly possible," Mac shouted as he ran from the room to escape Ted's vitriol.

Ted leaned back after the commander had gone.

"Where are we, Plato, on that reprogramming?" Ted asked.

"Almost there, my friend," the AI replied.

"Looks like we'll have time to streamline the code for the whole system. Let's pull that up and get started." Ted disappeared within the holographic representation of the gravitic shield application.

## Keeg Station

"What do you mean, no more suits?" Terry asked for the second time. His face twisted in frustration, not anger. He held his hands out in a calming gesture. He didn't need the people on the station to be afraid of him.

"Our resources are out there working on your ship. You get these four, which brings your inventory to twelve, but we can't manufacture suits and repair the *War Axe* at the same time. Our structural resources are stretched thin. We'll work on more suits once you've deployed again," the station's logistics chief explained patiently.

"I understand, Daniel. We all do the best we can with what we have." Terry looked at a box that appeared in the chief's hands. He was all smiles.

Terry raised his eyebrows but didn't speak.

"Here you go, Colonel," Daniel said, turning the box and popping open the lid.

Two Jean Dukes Specials were nestled in soft fabric, with four magazines stuffed in around them.

"They are unkeyed at present. Take care of that as soon as possible. We don't need these falling into the wrong hands."

"I know a couple warriors who will greatly appreciate these." Terry smiled broadly, showing his straight, white teeth while never taking his eyes from the pistols. He secretly called them the World Enders, because of the power they could unleash. "Thanks for everything you do, Daniel."

Terry wanted to end on a high note. He was disappointed that he'd only get four more mechs, but with the addition of two JDSs, it almost made up for it.

Almost.

Terry waved as he left the quartermaster's office. He walked through the mostly empty corridors of Keeg Station. It was a working station where most personnel had something to do. Some children played tag on the promenade, the shopping area. A food shop rolled its door into the ceiling, the proprietor hoping the smell of his fare would entice the early diners.

Foliage trailed throughout, flowers blooming from hanging pots. Terry stopped by the small restaurant with the open door.

"Come in!" the man called out pleasantly as he rushed from table to table, straightening condiment bottles. "You are our first customer and that is always good luck, or so they say."

Terry looked at a figure in the back hunched over a portable computer. "How can I be first?" Terry asked.

"Him?" The owner pointed at the figure. "He never leaves. Says he writes books."

The owner waved dismissively with one meaty hand. "What would you like? Everything is fresh!" the man claimed.

"What kind of food do you serve?" Terry asked, looking around. Nothing gave away the theme. It looked like a typical dive.

"The only thing we serve here in Click, Click, Boom is Seppukarian food. It has an interesting blend of spiced meats in a heavy gravy over something that looks like rice to Earthers. It'll either put hair on your chest or give you explosive diarrhea. You can never tell which until after you've tried it. Seppukarian. It's a rite of passage."

Terry twisted his nose and curled his lip. Char refused to enter the place because she considered it an assault on her delicate senses. Once inside, Terry found that he couldn't disagree.

"I think I'm good, thanks, but I expect some of my people will make their way here. They are all about rites of passage, whether they make sense or not. It's something I would have done when I was a bit younger, about a hundred and seventy years ago."

Terry waved nonchalantly as he turned to walk out. He cast one last glance at the author, pecking away at his keyboard. Terry thought for a moment about introducing himself, but expected the man was oblivious to all around him.

And Terry couldn't be sure of the last time the author had a shower.

TH shook his head as he left to find Marcie and Kimber, the box carrying two Jean Dukes Specials cradled lovingly under his arm.

**The *War Axe***

"Smedley, call Nathan," Ted ordered.

"Belay that, Smedley," the captain replied. "We have to fly the dumbed-down version so no one knows this is a Federation warship."

"THAT'S INSANE!" Ted screamed, spittle flying from his mouth. "I will fix that right now, because Felicity won't let me put our friends at risk. If Felicity found out, there would be hell to pay. Smedley, call Nathan, right now."

Micky raised his hand to object a second time, but he knew that Ted was right. It was the argument that he'd raised when they left space dock before the ship was finished because Bethany Anne was taking her armada to Earth and wanted the *War Axe* for the mission that would be Terry Henry and the Bad Company.

"Nathan Lowell," the voice said as he tried to figure out who had called him. "Ted, is that you?"

"You sent this ship to war and you wouldn't let them use the latest technology? If I tell Felicity, you'll be in big trouble."

Nathan stared at the screen, wondering about Ted's tirade. "Okay," he said noncommittally.

"I don't care what you say, I'm not sending my friends out there like this. Not again. Never again."

"Or Felicity will kick my ass?" Nathan pondered with a half-smile.

"There will be a long line of people with Felicity at the front and I'll be right beside her!" Ted stood and stuck his chest out, glaring at the screen.

"I was wrong in trying to hide the origins of the Bad Company's Direct Action Branch. I think the value of the reputation alone will help calm things in the entire sector.

The fact that the *War Axe* came from the Federation will be the worst kept secret across twelve parsecs. Go ahead and top it off, Ted. If you know of any new technology that Team BMW is working on that could benefit the *Axe* and her passengers, install it. Understand?"

"I don't care what you say, Nathan, I'm going to install the latest technology in the *War Axe* and make it the best combat ship there is," Ted declared as he slammed his fist on the table.

"I think that's what he's saying…" Micky offered, but stopped when Ted glared at him.

"We're all agreed. Accept my apologies for the subterfuge, Micky. But there's one very important thing here. With the technology upgrade, the *War Axe* cannot fall into enemy hands, no matter what. If it looks like that will happen, Smedley will suicide and take the ship with him." Nathan leaned close to the screen to make it clear that he was deadly serious.

"You can't kill Smedley," Ted replied, frowning.

"Then you need to keep the ship out of anyone else's hands. If that's all, I'm off to check on the latest Pepsi shipments." Nathan's visage disappeared from the screen.

Ted looked like he wanted to call him back.

"Time to go to work, Ted. We have a ship to upgrade, you, and all of us. The technology is here. We only need to integrate it into the operations. And Terry Henry has no patience beyond five days, so that's our window. The bots and structural crews are recovered from the outside. The space around the ship is clear. First order of business is to bring up the gravitic shields."

Ted continued to look angry.

"Ted. Let's get to work," the captain declared in a low voice through gritted teeth.

"But…" Ted started to say.

"We're going to fix it, Ted, all of it, and it won't fix itself. We need you," Micky said more softly, starting to understand how best to deal with the genius werewolf.

"Plato, take over the maintenance bots and send them to the gravitic shield projectors. Prepare to run diagnostic Ted Six Alpha," Ted stated clinically, his face set as the exchange of the last few minutes was forgotten and he focused unerringly on the task at hand.

# CHAPTER FIVE

"Fuck me! One more day? Come on, Micky, the people of Alchon Prime are running out of food. How much longer is this going to take?" Terry blew out a long breath and closed his eyes in a feeble attempt to avoid getting angry.

"Ted needs it to finalize some things, and for the record, he's going with us to keep working with the ship."

"How broke was the *War Axe*?"

"In more ways than you'll ever know, but what matters is that the alien fleet won't know what hit them. You won't be able to recognize the ship," Micky said, before looking away. "Get out of here, you mangy beast!"

Micky jerked in his chair as he kicked at something that Terry couldn't see.

"We need to get going, Micky. Is there any way Ted can do what he needs to do while we're underway?"

"WENCESLAUS!" Micky yelled before covering his nose. "That cat will be the end of me. And no, TH. Ted is upgrading the engines to their full capability, so we can't move until they're ready. Once that's done, it will expedite our trip in-system, so we'll be able to make up some time. It will also increase our survivability. We want to make sure you have a ship to come home to at the end of every op. Ted seemed to think Felicity would have our asses if we let you get hurt."

"That's Ted's way of saying he cares," Terry offered before pursing his lips. "We'll bring everyone aboard later today so we'll be ready whenever the ship can deploy. I promise that we'll stay out of your way, Micky."

"You need to stay out of Ted's way, if you know what I mean." Micky chuckled quietly to himself. Ted elicited a wide range of emotions in everyone with whom he interacted. Micky decided then and there that Felicity was a saint.

"You got that right. You should have known him before he got married, when he was the alpha of a wolf pack."

"I thought Char was the alpha?" Micky looked confused.

"Char is the alpha of the werewolves. Ted had a pack of wolves, I mean real wolves. Anywhere from ten to twenty-five of them. It was the craziest thing. He'd go to war if anyone threatened his pack, but we'd be in the middle of a firefight and he'd check out, start doing something else. That was crazy, too. He doesn't go into combat with us anymore. We decided that was best for everyone," Terry explained.

Micky nodded. "We'll see you later then, TH. Gravitic shields are offline. Contact Smedley when you are underway and he'll make sure the hangar bay is ready to receive the drop ships."

"Gravitic shields?"

"Like I said, you won't be able to recognize the *War Axe*. What a beautiful ride we have. And deadly, too."

"I like it, but please, no more than one day, Skipper. The people of Alchon Prime are counting on us. See you in a few. Walton out."

## Keeg Station

"Kimber, have the platoon form on the hangar deck for immediate return to the *War Axe*. Marcie, round up the rest of the derelicts and get them on the drop ship," Terry ordered.

"Derelicts? You mean your kids and the pack?" Marcie replied, shaking her head.

"I thought it was pretty clear." Terry looked at Char for confirmation, and she nodded in agreement. Terry wasn't sure what she was agreeing to. He didn't bother clarifying.

"Thanks for the thunderstick, TH," Marcie added, tapping the JDS secured at her side.

Kimber caressed hers, grinning. "Kae is so jealous."

"He's got a mech platoon. What's he jealous of? One little pistol?" Terry winked at his daughter.

"He's just mad that I got mine first. Sibling rivalries seem to go on forever. Thanks. Now, I'm one up on him."

"Use your power for good, not evil," Terry admonished by giving her the thumbs up and a big smile.

Marcie headed out to find the tactical teams to get them packed and on their way to the shuttles. Kim punched her dad in the shoulder, before following her sister-in-law out.

"What was that for?" Char asked.

Terry shook his head.

"Another day? Don't let it give you a coronary, lover," Char said softly. "You know Micky wouldn't do it if it weren't necessary. And it has Nathan's support because Ted is involved. He doesn't work for the Bad Company, only Team BMW now."

"Necessary or not, we have a mission to complete. I hate to fail and feel like I've lost this one before we even started."

Char put a hand on his shoulder. "I know," was all she said, but her look of sympathy and her sparkling purple eyes told him all he needed to hear.

## The *War Axe*

Terry stood in the hangar bay as the last of the drop ships slid through the energy screen, slowed to a landing within the bay, and oriented itself for a return to its launch tube. It taxied in, hovering slightly above the deck using its gravitic thrusters to push it home. The ramp dropped and Timmons staggered out.

"What the hell?" Terry grunted.

"If you get to know the people at Seymour Heine, then you can have a good time without beating anyone up," Timmons slurred.

"How can you be drunk?" Terry wondered, leaning close to look into Timmons's yellow eyes. The pupils weren't dilated.

"Not drunk. Haven't slept in three days. Sue and I are looking forward to some groovy sleep time during the cruise."

"Groovy sleep time," Terry repeated, stepping back and

jamming his fists against his hips. "Do the words 'mission prep and training' mean anything to you?"

"At the moment? Not a whole lot. We'll see you in the morning, TH. You be cool, bro." Timmons sauntered away with his arm draped over Sue's shoulders. Shonna and Merrit waved as they walked past. Christina waved with one hand as she held her head with the other. She stumbled by, following Shonna and Merrit to the hatch leading to the interior of the *War Axe*.

Aaron and Yanmei stopped in front of the speechless Terry Henry Walton.

"Cat got your tongue?" Aaron asked. Yanmei giggled.

Dokken strolled up and sniffed Terry's leg. He reached a hand down to scratch the German Shepherd behind his big ears.

"I think that I'm going to have to cancel liberty for the Bad Company for the rest of your natural lives," Terry declared as he hammered his fist into his hand.

Aaron raised his eyebrows. "It's too late for the natural lives thing, TH. We are well into the unnatural thing now. Did Ted ever get that comm system working for a direct link back to Earth? We'd like to talk with our kids, if we could, and soon would be great. It's been too long, TH."

Terry and Char both frowned. "I know what you mean. We'd like to check in on the grandkids. That makes us sound old, but I don't care. I want to know that they're doing okay."

Aaron and Yanmei started to walk past, then stopped. "We're not going to be dumped into the middle of a civil war again, are we?"

"Not this time, and if I have my way, not ever again.

That was some serious bullshit. This one is about breaking a blockade, so I may have to put on my diplomat hat and talk with them," Terry replied.

Aaron smirked, then started to chuckle. "Good luck with that! Sounds like we'll be throwing down before you can say Bob's your uncle." Aaron was shaking his head as he walked away, holding hands with Yanmei.

"I'm not that bad, am I?" Terry asked Char, his brow furled.

"You're the one who said he was going to burn the fucking president's palace down. I think you're also the one who shakes people by their necks when they're being stupid."

"But they're being stupid and aren't listening to reason," Terry countered, trying to look innocent.

"And that's why we all love you, Terry. We know where you're coming from. I think that I would be afraid if you were able to tolerate mealy-mouthed diplomatic double-speak and duplicity," Char offered with a loving smile. "But these are aliens. We have no idea what motivates them in order to negotiate. We will see soon enough, but you know what you say."

Terry had a tendency to philosophize a great deal, so he couldn't be sure to what his wife was referring. He shook his head and held up one hand.

"Walk softly and carry a big gun," she clarified.

Through the open hangar bay door, Keeg Station floated in all its glory, not even a speck of light from the nearest shipping lane. Terry turned to look at it.

"Home," he muttered.

"We've lived in worse places," Char offered as she

reached around Terry's narrow waist and pulled him close to her. They stood silently watching the nearby station.

A heavy metallic tread forced them to turn. Four powered, armored suits stopped and faced them. The back popped on one and Kaeden climbed out.

"Taking the new suits for a test drive," he said casually. He stabbed a thumb over his shoulder. "You guys want to run them through their paces?"

"We have such good kids, don't you think?" Terry said, before offering a hand to power-shake with his son. They grinned and grunted as they tried to out-shake the other before both surrendered.

"That's enough, boys. Yes, Kae, we'd be more than happy to give the suits a test drive, but who are the suits going to be assigned to?"

"I think these will be multi-use, based on mission para-meters. Looking at what we have so far, I think we may need them for stealth insertion of the tactical team."

Terry had been thinking the same thing, but didn't want to commit to one course of action over another before they arrived in the Alchon System and saw the battlefield firsthand.

"We may, so, yes. We'd love to take these for a test drive." Terry grinned before leaning conspiratorially close to Kaeden. "Do you know what the hell happened to the pack? They look like shit."

"I do," Kae replied before walking back to the mech fireteam and chasing one of the warriors out of a second suit. "They are all yours, Dad. I need to get back in there and check on the other suits and start working up a training plan for a twelve-person mech platoon, three squads of four. No rest for the weary."

Terry looked at Char. "He didn't answer my question."

"He most certainly did. You need to ask better questions, but if you had, then he probably *would not* have answered it. Some things are better left unknown, lover," Char replied. She picked one of the suits and started to climb in. The shipsuits they wore made for easy integration with the armor and she was inside and buttoned up before Terry could reply.

He shrugged, knowing that she was right. He took the suit Kaeden had brought and climbed in, breathing deeply of the new car smell. He settled in, buttoned up, and ran through the suit's diagnostics.

"It's show time," he said in a low voice to the other three mechs.

---

"I have to go," Ted said, waving one hand dismissively as the person on the other end of the line was speaking nonsense. "And I have no idea when we'll be coming back."

"I love you, Ted," Felicity said, looking at Ted from the screen.

"Me, too," was the most he would say. Her eyes glistened with the start of tears. Ted bit his lip and started to shake. He couldn't handle it when Felicity cried. "I have to go. I'll be in touch as soon as I know anything."

Ted signed off, but kept looking at the blank screen. "I love you, Felicity. Thank you for believing in me," he whispered, before his face hardened and he stood to leave. He stopped and looked around the space that he'd claimed for his lab. Blank gray walls stared back at him. A computer system with an immersive holographic station occupied the center of the space, with a small terminal beside it for mundane use, like speaking with his wife.

To Ted, the space wasn't austere. It had everything he needed.

*Terry Henry,* he said, using his comm chip. *Call Felicity and reassure her that you will make sure that I get home safely.*

<hr />

Captain San Marino sat in his chair watching the bridge crew run through a series of diagnostics and simulations. Clifton, the helmsman, was practicing flying with the new engines. The responsiveness was both exciting and terrifying. Before, he had time to react, but now, the new flight profile made things happen at a much quicker pace. But he was a pilot and flying was something he reveled in, despite the size of the *War Axe.*

Micky winced when the helmsman crashed the virtual ship into a virtual asteroid. Clifton reset the simulation and looked shocked that the captain had seen him. Micky pointed to his own eyes and then at the helmsman. *I'm watching you.*

Clifton returned to his simulation and on the second pass, he gave the asteroid a wide berth as he smoothly navigated through a virtual asteroid field.

"Gravitic shields?" Micky asked, looking to K'Thrall.

"Shields are available at one hundred percent functionality," the Yollin reported. "Weapons systems are at one hundred percent, pending final verification of alignment."

"Very well," Micky replied. Two others tested bulkheads and airlocks. They both gave a thumbs up before Micky asked. He could see the green lights dancing across his status panel.

"Smedley, get Ted on the line, please."

"I don't understand why you use that phraseology, Captain. There is no line," Smedley replied. The captain waited.

"Yes, Smedley?" Ted's voice sounded through the speakers.

"Captain San Marino here, Ted. What's your status?"

"I'm currently interrupted," Ted stated matter-of-factly.

Micky groaned. "I should have known better. My apologies, Ted. Can we take the ship out and test fire the mains?"

"Yes, yes, all of that. Let me know before you want to gate. Plato and I are making some adjustments."

Micky looked at his panel. "I didn't know you were doing anything with the gate engines," Micky said coldly.

"They needed to be fixed in case we have to leave a place quickly. When I'm done, we'll be able to do that, no matter how far we are inside the gravity well or what's going on around us. By my calculations, we'll cut down the time to establish a gate by seventy-four percent."

"Holy shit," Micky blurted. He wasn't a fan of people messing with his ship, but then again, this was Ted, and he was making the *War Axe* into a preeminent combat vessel. That could run away quickly if it had to. Micky didn't want to get captured and force Smedley to suicide, taking the ship with him.

"I'll let you know when we're ready, Ted." Micky signed off. "Smedley, give me ship-wide broadcast please."

"Of course, Skipper," Smedley replied.

"Smedley, you are spending far too much time with TH."

"Time is an investment. I look at it as time well spent. I've been helping them with their combat preparations using their mech suits in a zero-gravity environment," Smedley explained.

"This makes me wonder if I know anything that is going on around here."

"Terry Henry Walton uttered those exact same words," Smedley replied.

"I suppose you know everything that's going on," the captain said.

"Within my capacity, yes. I have to admit that some of the things that Ted and Plato are doing elude my understanding."

"What Ted does eludes everyone's understanding." Micky leaned back and pointed one by one to each member of the bridge crew. They replied with nods and thumbs up gestures. "Prepare to get underway, thrusters only, destination, asteroid firing range four alpha."

"Preparing to get underway, aye!' Clifton shouted.

"All green for standard movement," Smedley replied. "Ship-wide broadcast is open."

"Good morning, crew and passengers of the *War Axe*. We are preparing to get underway, with our first stop being the asteroid field to align our main weapon systems.

After that, we'll be gating directly into the Alchon heliosphere, where we have a blockade that demands our attention. The people of Alchon Prime are counting on us to open up the shipping lane to restore food and other shipments. We need to stay on our toes, because we have no idea how the alien fleet will react to our presence, but we have some new tricks up our sleeves. Make final preparations to get underway. Department heads, report."

One by one, the commanders delivered their status. Within twenty seconds, the board was a final green.

"Take us out, helm."

# CHAPTER SIX

Terry, Char, and Dokken walked through the corridors of the *War Axe* on their way to the mess deck. "I don't know what it is about being on a ship that makes me so hungry," Terry lamented.

"You're always hungry," Char retorted, but she didn't hold him back. She was a willing conspirator in reducing the food stock on board the *War Axe*.

*Me, too,* Dokken panted as he ran along. He stopped, sniffed, and started to bark. He took off down a transverse corridor, baying like a coonhound as his paws ripped at the deck.

"We're going to eat without you!" Terry yelled after the dog. Dokken was incensed and had Terry tuned out. "Maybe I should go after him."

Char stopped. "What for?"

"Our arch nemesis!" Terry declared.

"You don't have an arch enemy. Either of you. I can't believe how a big orange cat is causing the two of you fits.

It's a cat, not enhanced, not sentient, as far as we know," Char said slowly, speaking clearly. "Just. A. Cat."

"He's our arch nemesis."

"By all that's holy!" Char punched Terry in the stomach with a blow that would have felled a lesser man.

"Hard as a rock!" Terry declared, smiling.

"Are we going to eat or stand here and wonder why a stupid orange cat is outwitting your sentient dog?"

*I'm not your dog,* Dokken replied into their minds. *He got away. Again. He has to be getting help from somewhere. I suspect that engine technician is doing more than she lets on. And those weretigers, too. They're shady.*

*The weretigers are not shady,* Terry replied, shaking his head. *Let's get some lunch. We can talk over our strategy for capturing our arch nemesis.*

"You don't have an arch nemesis. Neither of you!" Char stated, crossing her arms and glaring at her husband. Dokken trotted up, saw the look on her face, and kept running past.

"You little traitor," Terry called after the German Shepherd.

The ship vibrated with one rumble, then a second. After a few moments, the pattern repeated. Two minutes later, the vibrations stopped.

"I like it when they fire the mains." Terry smiled and closed his eyes. "Feel the power."

"They pack a punch," Char agreed. "I wonder when we are going to gate into the system."

"All hands, report to battle stations. Gating to Alchon in ten minutes," Micky told the ship.

Terry looked shocked and started running toward the stairs to the bridge. Char was close on his heels.

They took the steps three at a time as they continued upward, diving out of the stairwell on the bridge level. They dodged around two corners and raced onto the bridge. The captain and crew were engaged in verifying that the ship was ready to create the gate and jump into the Alchon System.

"I need more time," Terry said without preamble.

Micky hesitated before looking up. "I thought you wanted to get there as quickly as possible. Ted got us ready early."

"You said we had another day," Terry countered.

Micky didn't dignify that with a response. "How long before you can be ready?"

Terry hung his head, his cheeks flushed with embarrassment. "Give me an hour to rally the troops and prepare for combat. We could vault right into the middle of the shit, right?"

"Yes," Micky replied, before tapping the panel on the arm of his chair. "All hands, we will gate one hour from now. Mark."

Terry nodded. "Thanks, Micky."

*Marcie, all hands on the hangar deck in ten minutes. Kae, get all twelve suits ready and climb in. Timmons, get the pack there. Full weapons load and tactical kit, people. Shit's about to get real, and it won't be anything like what we found on Poddern.*

Terry pointed to Micky. "See you on the flip side, my man. We'll be in the drop ships and ready to do whatever. We'll monitor from there."

"My intent is to cruise the line and assess their capability while trying to look non-threatening. If they force our hand, well, we'll cross that bridge when we come to it," Micky offered.

"You are the man, Skipper." With that, Terry and Char walked off the bridge. Dokken had been waiting in the corridor since the door closed before he could get inside.

"Come on, buddy. We're going to war," Terry told the dog.

*What's new?* he replied.

---

Kimber had the platoon in formation, what was left of them after Kaeden had pulled people for his mech unit. That left barely more than two squads.

Bundin ambled about behind the platoon. The Crenellian, Ankh'Po'Rout, stayed near him. No one knew why. The two had been enemies until they were folded into the Bad Company.

Terry and Char walked through the hatch exactly ten minutes after they had given the order. Terry was happy to be the last ones there. He hated seeing any of the warriors arrive late. Even the pack was in line beside the platoon. Twelve mechs stood tall behind the formation.

Christina was beside Timmons, whispering something his way. He chuckled briefly, before recovering and trying to look somber.

Ted appeared behind Terry and Char. He brushed past and headed straight for the Crenellian. He and Ankh talked briefly and then they both hurried away.

Terry turned to Char.

"Before you ask, no. I have no idea what that was about," Char stated preemptively.

"Time to do my thing?"

Char nodded and smiled, shoving her husband forward with a gentle push to the small of his back.

Marcie called for quiet and all eyes locked onto Colonel Terry Henry Walton.

"It's that time, people. Time to go back to doing what we do best—bringing justice to the universe." Terry looked at the grim faces. No one cheered. They didn't need cheerleading, only the details of the mission, including the mission objective. They'd already been briefed repeatedly, but this was Terry's opportunity to leave them with final thoughts before they jumped into the crucible.

"We need to break a blockade and all we have is the *War Axe*. If we need you to do damage control, you do damage control. If you have to block an atmospheric leak with your body, you do that. We will do anything and everything to stay in the fight, because we can't win the fight if we're not in it. We may have to do some stealthy infiltration. I have an idea what that looks like, but I'm just like you. I've never done it before, but if we have to, we're going to make it look like we're old pros.

"No matter what, we have to clear the blockade, because the people of Alchon Prime are counting on us. If we are unsuccessful, then they start dying. I can't have that. We can't have that. Check your weapons and load up. If anything happens to the *Axe*, we're taking the drop ships right down their throats and we'll enter their ships any way we can. Then we wreak havoc, and they'll rue the day they crossed the Bad Company."

Terry pointed to Marcie and twirled his finger. He then pointed at Timmons and signaled for him to join Terry.

Christina came along too, as well as Bundin. Terry looked at the Podder.

"I can help," Bundin said aloud.

"Sonofabitch!" Terry exclaimed. "That was weird. I thought I heard you with my ears."

"You did. I have an external speaker attached to the bottom of my shell," Bundin replied.

"Sonofabitch!" Terry grinned at the blue, stalk-headed Podder. "How can you help us?"

"I can operate in space without a suit. I can help you penetrate an enemy ship without them knowing that I am there."

"How do you know this?" Terry was skeptical. The Podders were barely industrialized and their only space travel had been from their relations with the Crenellians, which didn't contain two-way communication.

"A number of us were taken to space and shown the orbital weapons systems. There was an accident and a couple of my people were jettisoned into space. They survived easily and made their way back into the ship. We estimated that they were able to remain in space for up to thirty minutes without ill effects," Bundin explained.

"Holy shit!" Terry slapped the Podder's shell. "I like the hell out of that, Bundin. We may need you to repair this ship too, if we take any more hits like we did over Poddern."

Timmons and Christina arrived and waited patiently while Terry talked with Bundin. When he saw them, he excused himself, still scratching his head over the revelation that the Podders could survive in space without an environmental suit.

"You called, maestro?" Timmons asked. Char tipped her head and looked down at Timmons.

"Too much liberty for you?" she asked.

Timmons chewed the inside of his cheek. "What's the right answer where I don't get confined to the ship whenever we get a chance for more time off?" he replied.

"Get yourself under control. You can't show up for a mission looking like you're on your death bed!" Char blurted. At one point, she'd had to cut off Timmons's hand to make her point about who was the alpha and who did as the alpha directed. He had never forgotten that lesson. It took getting horribly burned by acid to remove the silver that had kept his hand from growing back. He appreciated his return to being a fully intact werewolf.

"Point taken." He bowed before Charumati, sweeping his hand wide. "It shall be as you determine, my alpha."

"Once I find a boyfriend, I won't have to hang out with this mob of delinquents," Christina suggested, pointing with her eyes at Timmons. His lip curled of its own accord.

"A boyfriend?" Terry asked as he joined the conversation. "We can't be thinking about boyfriends. We're going to war."

Christina shook her head. "I'm not thinking about that at all. I don't have one. Honestly, are all men like this, only hear half of what you say?" Christina looked at Char.

"Not all, but most," she replied, nodding toward TH.

He gave them both the stink-eye. "Christina. I need you to train up on the suits. You too, Timmons, and the pack, including the weretigers. Our twelve best in hand-to-hand

71

combat need to be able to use the suits to travel through space, manipulate tools, and bring down the thunder."

"I don't think Kae and his people will like that," Christina said, turning her head sideways to glance at the mechs as they performed their dexterity routine before climbing aboard the drop ships.

The Bad Company's Direct Action Branch always boarded the drop ships whenever they gated, just in case an enemy was waiting for them on the other side. The shuttles gave them an escape, a way to attack, a way to survive. At some point, Terry would revise the tactics, but not yet.

"No choice, Christina. If we're going to get into a throw-down with aliens, I need you there. I need the pack, and I need Marcie, Kim, and Kae. The deadliest among us will lead the way, as we've always done. From the days of the FDG until now, those with the superior abilities have the responsibility to lead the way, assume a higher level of risk. We'll swap with Kae and his people after we've gotten the lay of the land, so to speak. For now, it's best that those most familiar with the suits stay in them, but get ready to swap out and train as soon as humanly possible."

"Will do," Christina and Timmons replied together.

"Can you let Kae know, to lessen the friction?" Timmons added.

"He already knows." Terry was all business. "The decision is made and at this point, it's about following orders. Get to your ships and get your people ready as we transit to Alchon space. I don't expect there will be anything for us, but you know how that usually works out."

Timmons started to laugh. "No plan survives first

contact, and this is a real first contact. We really don't know anything about this bunch running the blockade? Aliens, not aliens, nothing?"

"Nothing. It's up to us to figure it out *and* fix it."

"That doesn't instill confidence, TH." Timmons looked to Christina. The unknowns of the mission were reflected in her skeptical look.

"I'm not going to blow smoke up your ass. We don't know jack shit except that if the alien fleet is too much for us, we have to get Alchon Prime to request to join the Federation. Then General Reynolds can send a few dreadnoughts and battleships to give us a hand. That's our ace in the hole, assuming we can communicate with Alchon Prime when we get there."

Timmons looked like he wanted to say something else, but Marcie and Kimber were barking orders, sending the groups to their separate drop ships. The mechs took up a great deal of space and were given two ships just for them, while the rest of the Bad Company filled out the other four.

"Time to go, my friends," Char said as Terry watched the groups move to their assigned shuttles.

*Smedley, can you give the order for hoods, please,* Terry requested.

Almost instantly, over the hangar bay's loudspeakers bellowed General Smedley Butler's voice. "HOODS!" With well-practiced motions, as one, the warriors pulled their hoods from behind their necks and snapped them into place. Internal suit pressure filled them out and the group of bubble-heads continued unimpeded into their drop ships.

Terry and Char bumped their bubbles, as they'd taken to doing whenever they pulled their shipsuit hoods up. They held each other and looked into each other's eyes through the clear hoods. They both mouthed, "I love you," and then they put on their war faces and went to work.

# CHAPTER SEVEN

"Bad Company personnel show green," Smedley reported.

The captain nodded. "Hoods, please," he said conversationally. The bridge crew pulled their hoods into place.

"The ship is green," Smedley verified.

"Ted?" Micky asked.

"We will gate to a point well within the heliosphere, one hundred thousand kilometers from the closest alien vessel. The sensors have been upgraded and will begin feeding data to the system immediately upon arrival. Gravitic shields are active and in place. Weapon systems are hot and will remain that way through the jump. Targeting is slaved to the bridge station for weapons release."

Micky whistled before smiling. K'Thrall turned his chair around to look at the captain. He'd been told what the upgrades would do, but hadn't believed it.

"I've never heard that any of that was possible, no matter the ship," the Yollin said.

"As a fleet that contains one ship, our survivability chances have vastly improved. Take charge of the weapon systems and prepare for defensive fire. The mains on my command only. We don't want to scare the aliens. Not too much, anyway."

Micky leaned back in the captain's chair. He looked from station to station, received the manual thumbs up, which he liked in addition to the status board that showed green.

"Commander Suresha?" Micky asked.

"Main engines are ready for maximum maneuverability. Gate engines are at capacity. On your command, Captain."

"Ship-wide broadcast, Smedley, count us down."

The EI's voice counted down pleasantly from ten to one, and then the gate formed in front of the *War Axe*. Clifton goosed the engines and the ship darted across the event horizon and through the gate.

The crew didn't feel the change. Technology protected them from the turbulence as the ship transitioned from normal space to the wormhole and back to normal space within the blink of an eye.

"Twenty alien ships on the screen in a rough ellipse around Alchon Prime. Two ships are on an intercept course. Their speed is increasing," K'Thrall reported.

"Move us away at an offset of ninety degrees. Don't show our ass to those things," Micky ordered. "Tactical display on the main screen, Smedley."

The positions of the planets and alien ships appeared at the front of the bridge.

"What are those ships on the perimeter of the heliosphere?"

"Those are transports and cargo ships who are on the

wrong side of the blockade," K'Thrall replied. "And those green blips around Alchon Prime are friendlies stuck on that side."

"At least the aliens are leaving them alone. Let's join our fellows at the edge of interstellar space."

"Aliens are firing."

Micky lurched forward in his seat. "Brace for impact!" he shouted over the broadcast.

"It's an energy beam of some sort. The gravitic shields shunted the beam away from us, but not without losing some of their power," K'Thrall intoned. "Aliens are firing again."

Micky didn't issue a second warning.

"We are caught in a crossfire. The energy beams are electromagnetic pulses, EMPs."

"ENOUGH!" Micky roared, giving up on outrunning the enemy ships. "Helm, bring us about. Prepare to fire the mains."

"Helm is coming about. Holy crap, this thing turns on a moonstone!" Clifton exclaimed.

"Weapons are true. I have the helm," K'Thrall reported as he took over attitude control to keep the main weapons aimed at the target. "Firing. Ten salvos away."

Micky watched as the enemy ships started to change course, but they were too slow compared to the *War Axe*'s main weapons, which fired super-heated plasma at nearly the speed of light.

The first three rounds missed, but the next seven walked across one ship, ending with a spectacular explosion. K'Thrall fired again. Ten more salvos in a computer-calculated arc across the projected flight path of the enemy ship. Only four plasma bolts hit, but that was enough. The enemy ship split in half, and flashes of light signaled the death knell. Darkness enveloped what had moments before been a vibrant bastion of life operating within the harshness of space.

"Get us out of here," Ted requested over the ship's broadcast. "Their weapon took the shields offline. I don't know why they're down, but if we take one more EMP hit, we'll be dead."

Ted's voice came through as an unemotional clinical analysis. The coldness of it shook the captain to his core.

"Helm, move us to a safe distance. Systems, are any enemy ships moving to intercept?"

"They are maneuvering, reducing the distance between their ships, but they are not closing on us."

"Very well," Micky replied as he stroked his chin. "Ted, how long do you think it'll take to repair the gravitic shields?"

"I just told you that I don't know why they are down. Until I can determine why, I can't tell you how long. I'm glad that I brought Plato along as he will help expedite the process, but if we're killed, we will lose not one, but two AIs. Whatever you do, Captain, please do not get us killed."

Micky looked in surprise at the arm of his captain's chair where the broadcast controls resided. "I will do my very best to keep us alive, Ted," he replied, trying not to sound sarcastic.

He knew Ted was being serious.

"Smedley, give me ship-wide," the captain requested while watching the enemy blips on the big screen. "Attention all hands. Our shields are down, and we are in the process of making repairs. Until they are operational, we will avoid all contact with the alien fleet. We are moving near the stalled shipping and will remain there for the near term. Keep your shipsuits on and be prepared to hood at any moment as you return to your normal duties. Captain San Marino out."

He tapped his access panel. "TH, meet me in my briefing room, please."

---

"Report to your damage control stations!" Terry ordered the members of the Bad Company. "And stay frosty!"

He usually added that as one of his favorite lines from *Aliens.*

"What do you think he wants?" Char asked as they watched the tac teams, mechs, and platoon members exit the drop ships.

"How do we fight these Fuckbert McAssholefaces?" Terry replied, scowling. "I have an idea or two. We'll need our people there too, if we're going to talk tactics."

Terry switched to his comm chip. *Timmons, Christina, Joseph, Marcie, Kim, Kae, and Aaron. Report to the captain's briefing room.*

Char nodded to the group as they approached. Dokken ran to greet them.

"Is it okay if we just walk with you?" Joseph asked. The others laughed or shook their heads.

"I'm still getting used to this thing," Terry said, tapping the side of his head with a finger.

"Your brain?" Timmons deadpanned.

"Very funny. Since I like you, I'll kill you last," Terry responded, making a pistol with his fingers and pointing it at the werewolf.

"In Timmons's defense, that's what I thought, too," Christina added innocently. "Aren't we supposed to report upstairs?"

"Rightly so." Terry and Char turned as one and strode toward the hatch leading from the *War Axe's* hangar bay. The group followed, with Yanmei and Petricia joining them as they always did. Cory, Ramses, and Auburn followed, too. Dokken weaved his way between the humans' legs as he worked toward the front of the crowd.

"The captain needs a bigger conference room," Char suggested.

Terry nodded, but didn't speak. He was already focused on the enemy. His mind raced through the possibilities. He hadn't been privy to the weapons that the aliens used, but he suspected that it was enough to drive the *War Axe* away. Terry listened as if he could hear how much the ship had been damaged.

And then he remembered what he forgot. He didn't have to guess.

*Smedley, what kind of damage did we take from the aliens?* Terry asked.

>>**The alien ships used an EMP weapon and caused our gravitic shields to fail. Ted is very concerned,**<< Smedley replied.

*No other damage besides that?*

>>**That was plenty, I assure you.**<<

*Thanks, General. Ted is on it, I suppose. Any idea when he'll have it fixed?*

>>**He does not have a repair estimate because he does not know how the damage was caused.**<<

Terry contemplated the answer as they climbed the six flights of stairs to get to the bridge level. He didn't come up with another question before they arrived.

One by one, they filed in. Terry stood to let others sit. Micky was already seated while K'Thrall stood. He was a four-legged Yollin, which made sitting in a human chair problematic. Joseph offered his chair to Petricia and Aaron offered his to Yanmei. Neither sat. Char stood as well.

The captain started to laugh. "Fine. Either we all sit or no one sits. Is this your way of telling me to get a bigger briefing room?"

Terry smiled and tipped his chin with a quick nod.

"Next time, we'll use the combat operations center, the COC on the third level. Next time. For now, let me show you what we have." Micky brought up the holographic display centered over the table that showed the Alchon System with the stylized graphics showing friendly and enemy forces.

Every face leaned in to study the graphic.

"Ted, do you have a status for us?" Micky asked loudly.

A disembodied voice responded, "No," followed by a crackle as the comm channel closed.

Terry and Char both chuckled. "Welcome to working with Ted," Terry said, before turning serious. "But what you get from him will be nothing less than the very best." Others nodded.

"Can you replay the engagement?" Marcie asked.

"Of course," Smedley replied over the speakers.

It started with their appearance through the gate,

approaching the alien ships at an angle. Then the maneuvering began, followed by the mains firing and destroying the two ships that had broken the picket to engage the *War Axe*.

"I like the main guns," Kaeden whispered to his sister. She smiled and nodded. The icon of the *War Axe* flashed yellow and then turned red.

"And that's when the combined effects of the EMP weapon finished our shields. At least their ships were dead by then. The others may have been too far away to detect that we were defenseless. In a relative sense, anyway. We're never completely defenseless," the captain added proudly.

Terry twirled a finger, asking for another replay. When that was done, he asked for another.

"What are you thinking, TH?" Marcie asked on behalf of everyone in the room. They weren't seeing anything new after the second replay.

"Back twenty seconds and re-run that." Smedley did as requested. "Again."

The clip replayed without Terry having to comment. He put his finger in the middle of the hologram to point out the actions of the aliens' capital ships within the blockade.

"See how they are getting behind their pickets, the smaller ships are like destroyers or cruisers. I'm not sure what they're called out here." Terry worked his way around the table to look at it from different angles. "Run it forward twenty seconds. Now loop from there to about thirty more seconds."

Terry pointed again. "These two ships are key. If we take them out, the others will run. I'd stake my life on it."

"Are you willing to stake the lives of all the people on Alchon Prime?" Joseph asked.

Terry parted his lips and whistled through clenched teeth. "We're already two days past when the food starts to run out. All those transports sitting outside the heliosphere… How long will they wait?"

Micky looked Terry in the eye. "Two have already left. Now that we're here, I think I can convince the others to stay around for a little while longer. New ships inbound have diverted."

Terry hung his head and closed his hands. "Starvation is no way to die," he whispered. He looked around the room, his eyes turning cold. "Options, people."

"We talked about infiltration using the suits. Can we make a high-speed pass where twelve of us drop off the hull when we get close or do a combat jump out the bay door?" Kaeden asked.

"They'd spot the suits. If they hit them with an EMP, we'd die, floating in space," Kimber replied.

"Ted gave me a bunch of stealth packs, a small device that clips on the outside of the suit, renders it invisible to electronics and some visual searches. He said they were developed on something called R2D2."

Terry cocked his head and opened his mouth. Char gripped his arm before he could speak.

"Well done, Kae. That gives us a good option," Char said. "Other options?"

"Can we sit outside their range and bombard them with the mains?" Ramses asked. A couple people nodded.

The captain shook his head. "All they'd have to do is come after us and we'll be finished. I don't see them sitting back and waiting to die. If they killed our engines and tried to board us, Smedley would be obligated to suicide to prevent the new technology from falling into enemy hands."

Terry leaned back and looked at the ceiling. Kae rolled his head as if he was being tortured.

Joseph looked unfazed. "The end of the Bad Company's Direct Action Branch in one fell swoop," he intoned. Petricia punched him in the arm.

Aaron leaned forward. "Hit and run with a delivery of suited warriors. Maybe we can conduct a little attrition warfare while using subterfuge as our main weapon."

Terry did a double-take. "Aaron? Who replaced our Aaron with this staff officer?"

"I watched an R. Lee Ermey movie while on the station," Aaron said with a sly tilt to his head.

"I'm not buying it, but that's the best plan yet. Anyone else?"

"When can we call in the Federation's dreadnoughts?" Auburn asked.

Micky shook his head again. "We can't call for reinforcements unless Alchon Prime requests to join the Federation. They can't do that because there's a whiteout over the planet. We think the aliens are conducting some kind of localized jamming. We can't talk to the planet, and they can't talk to us. We are both on our own."

"What's it going to take to execute a high-speed pass?" Terry asked the captain.

"Smedley, draw up an ellipsis at an offset angle of thirty degrees, closest point of approach of one hundred thousand kilometers. We break away at that point and the suits detach. They will continue traveling on the original trajectory while we increase speed to maximum to power away from the engagement. We'll take a couple shots at their big ships right before we turn. Show us that course of action on the holo display," Micky requested.

The icons reset. The *War Axe* moved from its current position in a lazy turn before accelerating directly at one of the aliens' capital ships. The *War Axe* turned tightly and darted away before getting too close. The plasma rounds tracked toward the enemy, but Smedley presumed that they wouldn't hit. The holo image enlarged, showing twelve silver specks drifting through space toward the alien blockade.

"Are you sure those stealth modules work?"

"Ted says they do," Kae replied.

Terry looked uncomfortable, like he'd eaten something that didn't agree with him.

Or maybe it was the risk he was being forced to swallow. Slow and steady wouldn't win this race. He needed to break the alien blockade if the people of Alchon Prime were to eat.

CHAPTER EIGHT

**Keeg Station**

Felicity stood in her office, looking at the stars through the transparent aluminum that passed for a window.

The comm device on her desk buzzed. She ignored it. Ted and the others had been gone for mere hours, but it felt like days. Everyone had gotten back together, in one place, and proved that where didn't matter.

Only the company one kept.

New Boulder to North Chicago to San Francisco to the stars. The group had been together for as long as she cared to remember. What went before she met Billy Spires and Terry Henry Walton was ancient history, dust in a book that would never get opened.

Her life with Billy had been good, but life with Ted had been better, because he didn't interfere with her being the mayor. He didn't need to be in charge. He preferred things the way they were. And he was a good lover.

Everything she wanted, but they'd gone off to war, as they were wont to do.

"You fix that ship of theirs and come home to me in one piece, do you understand me?" she asked the window, expecting that the hairs on Ted's arm would stand up, wherever he was.

## The *War Axe*

Ted stood in the middle of a holographic display of the coding used to drive the gravitic shields. He appeared to have more than two arms as he tapped virtual points in a three-hundred-and-sixty-degree circle around himself. He maintained a constant dialogue with Plato, his R&D AI.

Terry and Char watched him, wanting to interrupt to determine the status of repairs, but knowing that doing so would delay what they wanted. Ted wasn't playing a game. He was fixing the ship.

One of Ted's major failings was that he would forget to tell them when the gravitic shields were fixed. He'd move on to something else where casual observers wouldn't be able to tell the difference.

"Smedley, will you know when the shields are active again?" Terry asked the room in a low voice.

"Yes," Smedley replied. "Right now, they are reconfiguring the shields to jump-start them, if I heard the terminology correctly."

"Let us know, so we can start the countdown to launch. Do you have the flight plan programmed?"

"I have a number of variations prepared, including launch points for the mechanized warrior teams and the Podder."

"Who said Bundin was coming along?"

"Joseph ordered his inclusion in my planning. I believe Joseph and Petricia are working with Commander MacEachthighearna on a propulsion system that Bundin can carry so he can adjust his flight profile to match whatever the mechs do."

"In case our targets move and we can't maintain a ballistic trajectory, we'll need to use the suits' jets," Terry explained. "Where are they?"

"They are in the armored unit storage and maintenance area."

Terry and Char left Ted to his own devices. They wondered if he knew they had stopped by.

---

"Stop wiggling around," Joseph said, losing patience.

"Podders don't wiggle. We flow like wind-blown sand," Bundin replied. Joseph stopped and looked at his alien friend.

"Where do I look when I want to give you the hairy eyeball? Do I circumnavigate your shell and make sure that each of your four eyes gets equal time?" Joseph asked almost clinically while trying to do his best rendition of a Charumati stink-eye.

"Any one will do, although I can't fathom why I would deserve such treatment," Bundin replied in the low and rumbling rendition of his voice. "What does it mean, hairy eyeball?"

The Podder's stalk was hairless, as were his tentacle arms. The stalk protruded from the center of a shell below which were four stumpy legs. Podders had no hair.

"It's a human expression of disbelief."

"Ah." Bundin stopped moving and Joseph completed strapping the jetpack above the four waving tentacles.

"Here's how you activate it, with this button and these levers. It will push you, so make sure you are aimed where you want to go..." Joseph was explaining, when Bundin activated the device. Even at the lowest setting, it accelerated the Podder directly into the wall.

Bundin stabbed the button with one of the fingers at the end of a tentacle.

"You might want to wait until you're outside the ship before you ever do that again," Joseph said slowly and clearly.

"I believe I will." Bundin's mechanical voice was more subdued.

Petricia stood in a corner, watching the whole affair and shaking her head at her husband's new best friend. Hundreds of years old and never too aged to enjoy something in a new way.

A blue alien. Joseph saw her watching him and held out a hand, smiling as she took it, and they embraced.

---

"Where's my Crenellian?" Terry asked, looking around. "And as a matter of fact, where's my dog?"

*I'm not your dog,* Dokken replied from somewhere out of sight.

"I don't think he's your Crenellian, either. Marcie found him, but we don't keep other races as pets," Char replied.

*Hear, hear!* Dokken called out. They heard his paws

slapping the deck and the click of his nails as he trotted around a corner, tongue lolling, ears up, and eyes sparkling. Until he stepped on a glistening patch in the corridor where he started to slide, then slipped, then all four legs shot out sideways and he slammed into the deck.

He low-crawled forward until he was off the patch of ice. *Wenceslaus! I don't know how you did it, but this will earn you a beating the likes of which people will write songs about!*

"I'm pretty sure the cat had nothing to do with this, although I will concede that he is our arch nemesis," Terry offered as he studied the ice. "That took some engineering, and I can appreciate that, whoever the joker is. There will be payback, because I almost stepped on it. Thanks, buddy! You saved me from taking a digger."

*It's what I live for,* Dokken muttered.

Terry kneeled down to give both of the German Shepherd's ears a good scratch. Dokken's eyes rolled back in his head and his hind leg started twitching as Terry hit a good spot.

Char's eyes unfocused as she used her comm chip to ask Smedley where Ankh was.

>>He's in the lab with Ted,<< Smedley replied.

"We were just there," Char blurted aloud.

"Let me guess. Ted has him secreted away in his lair."

"Seems that is the case." Char smirked. *What's he doing, Smedley?*

>>He's rewriting a subroutine to Ted's specifications. He's almost finished. Standby.<<

Char held up a finger before Terry could ask.

>>They have finished what they were working on.

**Initial diagnostics suggest the gravitic shields are back online.<<**

Char's eyes shot wide before her face turned cold. "Shields are live," she said.

Terry stood up, much to Dokken's dismay, and with Char, they hurried to Ted's lab.

*Micky, it sounds like the shields are back online. We're heading to the lab now to confirm and get a timeframe for deployment,* Terry reported.

*We have multiple trajectories calculated and are ready to go when the word is given,* the captain replied.

Terry and Char burst into Ted's lab. Ted was immersed in his holographic display.

"TED!" Char bellowed. As the alpha, she had more influence on the werewolf genius than Terry. He was only a colonel, after all.

The holographic screens dropped and Ted turned. Dismay contorted his face. Behind him, wedged into a small space, was Ankh'Po'Turn, the Crenellian. He wore his usual blank expression as he worked with the programming screen.

"Are you done with the gravitic shields?" Terry asked, forcing himself to be patient.

"Done is relative. They are currently functioning. I cannot guarantee that they will continue to work should we be attacked by that EMP weapon again. I discourage further contact with this group."

Terry's jaw dropped. He could feel his temperature rising.

"That's not an option for us, Ted, but thank you for recommending it. We must clear this blockade so the people of Alchon Prime can get their food shipments and avoid death by starvation," Char offered calmly.

"Okay, then. I recommend eliminating those ships before they can use their weapon on us again."

"What was it? What did the aliens use on us?"

"Aliens? No. I don't think they are aliens. R2D2 has this type of research in the database. That's why I was able to fix it so quickly, but the repair is only temporary. The weapon is specifically designed to be used against Etheric-powered equipment, which means if the shields hadn't stopped it, anyone with nanocytes would have been affected."

"Affected how?" Terry pushed.

"As in all the nanocytes are rendered inert, albeit temporarily. As in if you get hurt during that time, you bleed and you die, just like any normal human."

"I can't remember what it's like to be normal. It seems like I've been enhanced my whole life. What would I feel without the nanocytes? And how did this bunch get R2D2 research?"

Char's jaw was set. "This changes everything," she whispered.

### A remote corner of the galaxy

Nathan held his head as he peered between his hands at Terry's report. "He called the enemy "Fuckberts," and they are using R2D2 technology." The head of the Bad Company scowled.

"Where in the holy hell would they get our technology?" Ecaterina asked.

"I don't know, but I think that revelation alone should make it feasible to bring in the Federation's big ships, a few dreadnoughts to scrape the scum off the bottoms of our shoes." Nathan leaned back so he could give his wife his full attention.

Her eyes fixed him in a steely gaze. "We have a leak."

Nathan nodded once and leaned back toward his screen. He tapped a couple buttons.

"Nathan. Judging by the look on your face, this isn't a social call, but since you didn't ask, I'm doing well. My last prostate exam suggested that I'm in perfect health!" General Lance Reynolds exclaimed as he chewed slowly on his cigar.

Nathan did a double-take. "You get prostate exams?" he asked without thinking. The general laughed and shook his head.

"Only trying to take the edge off whatever dire report you're going to deliver."

"Technology from R2D2 has fallen into enemy hands and they are using it against us at Alchon Prime. I think it's time to call in the cavalry, and we need to do a little soul-searching of our people working in R&D. The *War Axe* is out there right now and they are having some problems. Terry's people came up with a plan to infiltrate the alien ships, which they don't think are alien. I have no idea where someone could put together such a fleet without us knowing about it, but there you are." Nathan threw his hands up, disappointed that the ships had been built and launched without him having any idea.

"If I hear you right, you want me to send the Federation's biggest and baddest to deal with this threat to Alchon Prime?"

"Something like that, Lance. These are big ships, and although the *War Axe* is more than capable of protecting herself, the EMP weapon the enemy has could force Smedley into a position where he'd have to suicide and take the ship with him."

Ecaterina shifted uncomfortably before deciding to join Nathan where she could see the general.

Lance nodded to her when she appeared in the frame. "The Federation is expanding and with each new system comes new challenges. As we think we have a place secure enough to move on, some new warlord raises his ugly head, but that's nothing you don't already know. Why do you think Alchon Prime is more important than some other systems where we already have mutual defense pacts in place? I have to expend a certain amount of political capital if I'm to pull our forces out, so convince me why I should do that."

"Besides saving the *War Axe*, Terry Henry Walton, and the entire Direct Action Branch, we also have Ted on board with Plato. And Alchon Prime. We break the blockade, it's almost certain they'll request to join the Federation," Nathan explained.

"Fucking Plato? How in the hell did Ted get one of the R&D AIs onto the *War Axe*? Don't answer that." Lance removed his cigar and rubbed his chin while rolling the wet stogie between two fingers. "I can't guarantee anything."

"I can't let these Fuckberts get the best of us. We need to put them down. Hard."

"Fuckberts? Is that what we're calling them?"

"It's what Terry called them. Fuckbert." Nathan paused and grimaced. "McAssholeface."

"I gotta get better people." Lance rolled his eyes. "So the FMs, as we'll call them, have shown up with first-class warships carrying our research technology."

Nathan didn't answer. General Reynolds was thinking out loud and hadn't asked a question.

"You said Terry had a plan to infiltrate the enemy ships. Execute that plan and let's see if he can find how they acquired our research. And if he's resourceful enough to get on board their ships, then he'll be able to stop them from within. After he's done with them, if you still need Federation capital assets, I'll make a few calls, chew some ass on knuckleheads that like being carried, and see if we can get a dreadnought or four to Alchon Prime."

"The answer is no, then?" Nathan pressed.

"The answer is not yet." Lance maintained a neutral expression.

"I'll let them know that their infiltration mission is a go."

Lance gave a thumbs up and signed off without saying another word. Nathan wondered what else was going on in the general's world. Maybe he heard about the Pepsi shipment taking priority over the Coke imports.

He laughed to himself. The Federation occupied an immense section of space and trying to keep a handle on all of it, keep the members from revolting, took a force of will that Nathan could only marvel at. It made Alchon Prime and their human outpost seem trivial by comparison.

"The humans are on their own," Nathan told his wife.

"Seems so. Anything we can do?" Ecaterina asked.

"Keep the rest of the Federation from crashing down around our ears so Terry only has his one problem to worry about. I don't think that's unfair."

"No one's keeping count, Nathan, but that's two total fuck jobs in a row that you shoved Terry Henry's ass into. And our daughter too, if you're having a hard time remembering that. You will unfuck this and in a way that doesn't involve us becoming grieving parents. Do you understand me?" Ecaterina's jaw was set.

"I will fix it," Nathan said, having no idea how.

# CHAPTER NINE

**The captain's conference room, the *War Axe***

The enemy ships were presented in greater detail floating above the conference table. The holographic projection displayed them in a way that Terry could select individual ships, expand them, rotate them, and put them back where they were. He was doing that, one by one. The tac teams were wedged in around the table. No one attempted to sit.

"What are you thinking, Dad?" Kae asked.

"We have a couple choices and it all goes to how much we are willing to split the team. Thirteen of us on one target to maximize our chances of getting inside, or we split into as many as six teams to go after more ships, increasing the chance that we can take them out if we can't figure them out."

"There are two capital ships," Marcie said, pointing at the center of the enemy formation. "We break into two groups and take out their big ships, or we split into six and go after the two big ones and the next four largest. If we are successful with all six, that leaves a bunch of tin cans, destroyers, I think you called them."

"What can two people do on a ship that's bigger than the *Axe*?"

"You take me and you take Ankh. We can get into the system once we're on board, but we need you to get us safely there. That's not our shtick," Ted said from the back of the room.

"It is not," the Crenellian added. Terry couldn't see him behind all the bodies in the way.

"I'm not a fan of giving up two suits. We need the combat power, but I know that you're a force multiplier. Sounds like two teams and we go after their big boys," Terry replied.

Ted shouldered his way to the edge of the conference table. "Why not just tow extra people? We have shipsuits. How long do you think we'll be outside? Come on, TH. I don't see you wasting more than a few seconds. Calculating the trajectory, distance, time to open the airlock... Five minutes. We'll have plenty of time to spare."

Char, Kae, Marcie, and Kim nodded. The others in the room looked optimistic.

"Six groups of four and Bundin. Team leaders are me, Marcie, Kae, Kim, Christina, and Timmons. Smedley, follow along and calculate our release points. I'll take this one because I think it's their flagship. I'll take Ted with me. Marcie, you have the other capital ship and take Ankh with you." Terry pointed to the ships as he walked across the blockade. "Kim, Kae, Christina, and Timmons. Kim, you take Bundin, Joseph, Petricia, and Auburn. Ramses with me. Cory, you stay behind."

"She can go with me," Kae offered, but Terry shook his head. Cory didn't get angry. She hung her head.

"You're going to need me out there," she said matter-of-factly.

"I know we will, but we won't know which of the six ships will need you the most. You're better off here where you can react to the greatest need."

"You don't want me out there," she said softly.

Terry replied just as softly. "No, I don't. We've done some sketchy shit that we should not have walked away from, but this is probably the most dangerous. Not only are we hurling our bodies into the void of space, we're going after ships that have the capability to render our suits and our nanos inert. It only takes a couple minutes to die in space, no matter how you slice it. I've risked all of us for far too long. I won't do that anymore."

"Maybe it's not your choice," Marcie interjected, standing up straight, nearly as tall at Terry. "We're all volunteers, remember?"

"When it comes to combat, you know I don't fuck around," Terry retorted, flashing a snarl as he looked around the room, making eye contact with everyone who looked to him. "You stay here!"

"No," Cory replied. "I need to come. I'll join Kae's team."

Terry clenched his fist, not because he wanted to hit someone, but because he was losing the argument. He wanted her to come because she saved lives, pure and simple. She made sure people could get back into the fight. And once in a fight, she could hold her own. He rolled his head around his shoulders.

Char chuckled.

"What?" Terry demanded.

"You're so funny. You always want to change something, for the right reasons, and the wrong ones, too. Some decisions are out of your hands. Looks like we're taking a full load, twelve in powered, armored suits, twelve in shipsuits, and Bundin with his stalk-strapped jet pack."

Terry's jaw worked as he wanted to say something, but there wasn't anything that came to mind that didn't sound snarky or asinine. He settled on a different approach.

"Fuckberts won't know what hit them. Ted! How in the hell do we get on board their ship without them knowing about it?"

"If I knew that, we could simply send a drone," Ted replied with an eye-roll. "That's why I need to go along, but I can tell you that Felicity isn't going to be happy with you, Colonel Terry Henry Walton!"

The others turned away, but Terry could still hear their snickers. "You wouldn't."

"She's going to be mad at you, not me."

"Fine. Ramses, you stay within arm's reach of Cory at all times and keep her safe."

"I always do, Colonel," Ramses replied from where he stood at Cory's side.

"Suit up, people. Meet on the hangar deck in fifteen minutes. And, Ted, we're under full opsec, operational security, no calls leave the ship until the operation is over," Terry declared.

Ted looked at Terry as if he didn't comprehend.

"You can't call Felicity. No comms outside the ship," Terry reiterated.

"But I have to call her," Ted countered.

"Sorry, Ted. No calls."

"But I have to call her."

"SUIT UP!" Terry shouted, and the people started leaving the conference room. Ted stood dumbfounded. Dokken barked furiously and raced down the corridor.

Terry, Char, and Micky remained behind. "I wish I knew how that little bastard was getting into my quarters."

"Somebody iced down the corridor that I use."

"Someone hid all the chocolate ice cream," Char added. The two men looked at her. She shook her head and held her hands up. "It's not right."

"Can you deliver us on target? I'd hate to float past those ships and disappear into the cosmos. The people we'll be towing will have a limited air supply. I don't want to kill our people because we couldn't fly straight." Terry gripped the captain's shoulder as he bored into his eyes.

"We'll launch you on target. What I can't account for is if they move, which they are sure to do when we come racing in on our high-speed pass, but they returned to their starting positions last time, so that's where we'll deliver you. If necessary, you wait for them to come to you."

"That's a big 'if,' Micky."

"It's the best I can do for you. No promises besides that. If you need anything else from us, like a diversion, just let us know."

"Maybe a few streams of plasma to keep the ships where we want them," Terry suggested.

"I don't want to throw plasma past you while you're flying through space with nothing but a suit between you and incineration."

"Get ready to launch the drop ships to recover us. Or blast the aliens into non-existence if you haven't heard from us in twelve hours."

"Twelve? That's an awfully long time."

"Those are big ships." Terry finally let go of Micky's shoulder. "Stay frosty, Skipper."

Terry and Char walked out together. They could hear Dokken continue to bark, far in the distance. It remained unspoken that he couldn't come. Terry hoped he didn't have to look the German Shepherd in the face and tell him point blank that he couldn't come along.

"I like that dog," Terry said as they headed for the stairwell.

"Me, too," Char admitted.

---

Kaeden had brought his team directly to the armory where the mech suits were stored. Kae walked past each one, studying it before continuing on. The newest four, delivered by the Keeg Station production facility the past week, still smelled like they were fresh off the showroom floor. Flawless exteriors glistened with the room's lights.

Kaeden looked fondly at his suit. Creased, charred, scratched, and seared. It had undergone system repairs, but the cosmetics remained untouched. Salty, Terry had called it as a badge of honor. Some of the others, too.

Cantor's suit. He hadn't made it off Poddern alive. Fleeter had lost a leg. Even though that had been repaired by the nanocytes, she wasn't ready to deploy again. She was still getting regular treatments in the Pod Doc, but Kae wasn't sure what for.

He didn't press her on it. She had climbed into a super-tank and killed it, barely escaping after leaving her leg and a lake of blood behind.

He couldn't blame her for not being in a hurry to dive back into the fray.

Kelly and Capples were adamant about going. Kae took stock of the suits and counted those who wanted to wear them.

Terry, Char, Timmons, Sue, Shonna, Merrit, Joseph, Petricia, Kae, Marcie, Kim, and Ramses. The weretigers, Christina, Auburn, Cory, Ted, Ankh, and six or maybe seven more. That was it. That was all they could take with them to subdue an alien fleet.

Kae sighed as he caressed his suit.

"A dozen mechs capable of mass levels of destruction. If we had these back on Earth, we could have destroyed entire cities. But that's not our thing. Have them and not need them, like Fleeter, climbing out of hers to fight the battle within, the real battle. Any moron can hose down an area with a railgun," Kae told the empty suit.

"Any moron," Kim said from behind her brother. "Who are you talking to?"

She looked around and held up her hands when she didn't see anyone.

"No one." Kae stood up straight and took a deep breath before turning to Kim. "I don't have a good feeling about this."

"Who does? We are getting launched through space with the hope that we can get on board alien ships. Then we get to fight all of them. How many do you think are on board that big bastard? Do you think they're going to hand it over when they see us? Or maybe they'll fight like hellspawn because there is no place to retreat?"

"It does look grim," Kae conceded before smiling. "Isn't that our thing?"

"What's our thing?" Christina asked. She didn't wait for an answer before continuing. "Which suit is mine?"

"Umm," Kae stuttered.

She put her hands on her hips and tipped her head down to look at him.

"That one." Kae pointed to the suit he had dedicated to Petricia. He decided in that moment that Joseph would carry her since she hadn't trained in the mech simulator.

Kaeden didn't want to put anyone out, but he had way too many people and far too few suits. Someone was going to be left out.

They were all good with that because she'd saved Aaron's and Yanmei's lives. One for all, all for one, or so the saying went. Kae had no doubts that she would do the same for anyone else in the Bad Company. Neither did anyone else.

"You'll be carrying someone, as will we all."

"I know," Christina replied. She studied her suit for a moment, then turned to Kim and Kae. Her eyebrows knit as she frowned. "What are we going to find over there?"

"Selfishly? I want to find a door that opens and an atmosphere I can breathe, otherwise, I'm just going to blow the engines and get the hell out of there," Kim replied.

Kae held up his hand, and Kim slapped it.

"I approve that plan," Terry said loudly as he led the

group that would jump into empty space from a moving starship.

Terry turned so he could face the group. Were, vampire, enhanced humans, a Podder, and a Crenellian.

"Listen up, people. You've all been briefed, but let me break it down to its simplest elements. We jump off the *Axe*, fly to our targets, and try to board, unnoticed if possible. If we can get aboard, we try to find the heart and soul of the ship, the computer. Pop your hacker devices onto them so Plato and Smedley can get to work. If you have to take some of the aliens out, do so. If you can't find what you're looking for, blow the engines and get out of there. Use an escape pod or just jump and use the mech's jets to get you clear. I'm not so keen on taking prisoners, but if they surrender, zip tie them and move on."

"What if they can't be zip-tied?" Bundin asked, waving his tentacles.

"Then I guess we're fucked. Or not. Do your best with what you have, but remember, our primary mission is to break the blockade. Any questions?" The group shook their heads. Ted raised his hand, but Terry ignored him. "It's time to suit up and get to work."

CHAPTER TEN

The *War Axe* raced toward the enemy blockade, but turned to demonstrate that it wasn't attacking. It continued through a long arc as it approached the drop point for the Bad Company. The alien fleet started to move, but none of them brought their EMP weapon to bear.

"I don't think this was one of my best ideas," Terry mumbled. Twelve warriors in the powered, armored suits were magnetically attached to the rear of the sail, the section that stood above the *War Axe*'s superstructure. Each of the twelve held onto another person who was wearing only a shipsuit. One Podder used a tentacle to hold on to the ship while two people in suits were wedged against him, helping hold him in place.

Each of the twelve had a small box attached at their waists.

"You'll drop off at intervals of two to three seconds, be ready," Micky said through the helmet communications.

"Engage your stealth device," Terry ordered. The group

reached to the boxes and jabbed at the interface. It appeared as if nothing happened.

"Ted?" Terry wondered.

"You're invisible to electronic systems. You can still be seen by the naked eye," Ted replied dismissively.

"Trust the Force, Luke," Terry intoned.

"Team One, ready. Go," Smedley said, taking over the deployment because precision was critical. Two suited figures carrying two other bodies released their magnetic grapples and continued on a ballistic trajectory while the ship executed a long, lazy arc.

"Team Two, Go."

Smedley deployed the six teams, one by one. Terry and Char were the last to release. As they floated away from the ship, they both looked back to see the *War Axe* accelerating toward the pinpoints of light that were the cargo ships waiting at the edge of the heliosphere.

The only sound they could hear was their own breathing. Terry started to tumble.

"Stop squirming!" he said as he tried to head-butt Ted's bubble-head with his mech's helmet, but since Ted's was filled with air, it acted like a pillow, refusing to give TH his gratifying thump.

"Felicity is going to be pretty angry about this," Ted retorted, his face turning red.

"Stop telling me that you'll sic your wife on me. It'd be embarrassing for me to kick your ass in front of her."

"Ted, think about how you're going to crack the code to get through the airlock. The mission takes priority," Char said calmly as she maintained a firm grip on Cordelia.

At the last minute, Terry had put Ramses with a

different team. Ramses was upset, but if anyone would take care of Cory, it would be her parents. He relented when he found out that she was going with them. Ramses settled for getting carried by Kae.

"I expect that there won't be any codes to access the airlock," Ted admitted.

"No shit," Terry sighed.

---

Timmons tightened his grip on Sue. She looked at him through wide eyes that darted from his face to the immensity of space. "Follow me," Timmons ordered.

He touched his jets for less than a second as he forced his way off the ballistic trajectory. His target ship had moved, but it was still within a reachable arc, within the margin of error that Smedley had calculated for each team.

Shonna locked arms with Merrit as she tickled her jets to race after Timmons.

The werewolves bore down on the ship that Smedley had classified as a cruiser, the second largest in the alien fleet. Timmons checked his stealth pack to make sure it was still functioning. He wondered if Ted rigged the small green light. He had called it an idiot light when he briefed everyone on their use.

As long as the light was green, the suits were invisible to electronic discovery. Sue couldn't see the ship. Shonna held Merrit backwards so they could both see where they were going.

Sue closed her eyes. Her shipsuit was a too-thin barrier between her and the dead of space. She tried to calm her breathing to use less air and extend the amount of time they were able to search for and breach an airlock.

Timmons could sense his mate's unease. He wanted to caress her blonde hair, but he couldn't. He settled for focusing on getting aboard.

"We're coming in kind of fast, don't you think?" Shonna suggested. She was an engineer like Timmons and was critically studying the situation. According to her heads-up display, they were approaching at a speed of two hundred kilometers an hour.

"Oh shit," Timmons muttered before inverting and hitting his jets, staying on them until he slowed. Sue almost slipped from his arms. The panic in her eyes told him everything he needed to know. He locked his arms around her, which was what they had agreed to as SOP, but his mind had drifted. He grimaced and mouthed, "Sorry."

Her shock changed to anger. She glared at him through narrowed eyes until he looked at the approaching ship. He worked the jets until they slowed nearly to a stop. He didn't touch down on the ship as Shonna stayed a body's-length from him. He used the mech's maneuverability to survey the length of the hull, avoiding anything that looked like a porthole.

"Where in the hell is the airlock on this fat bitch?" Timmons muttered.

---

Joseph slowed his approach well before they reached the ship. Bundin used his stalk-strapped jetpack to keep pace. He twisted around, looking at space as the mouth-flaps at the top of his stalk remained tightly closed. Kim and Auburn had inadvertently floated ahead. At that distance, Joseph couldn't talk with them and could barely see them.

He waved at Bundin, pointed to Kim, and then motioned for him to follow. Joseph turned himself around and let his suit's jets rocket him toward the others on his team. He had to turn and slow before crashing into Kim and Auburn, who had stopped and were studying the massive ship before them.

"A battleship," she said to no one but herself. From the edge of the heliosphere, the ship had been nothing but a big target. Up close, it was an intimidating mass. One thousand feet from stem to stern. Although no weapons were visible, they knew it had to be armed with at least railguns to blast asteroids.

As were most ships designed for space flight only, the battleship wasn't sleek. It was boxy with protrusions, seeming like a squatter's paradise.

Need to add something? No problem, just stick it on.

"Over there," Joseph said softly. With one arm wrapped around Petricia, he pointed to an area where a circle of light highlighted an airlock.

Bundin activated his jetpack and sailed toward the hatch. Joseph hurried after him. Kim surveyed the ship around her before joining the others. Auburn watched it all happen. He was a passenger until he could stand on his own feet. He hoped that would be soon, and without alerting the locals.

Terry squinted as he tried to see the others, but they were lost in the darkness. "Might as well be invisible," he said.

Ted had turned around and was trying to look at the ship they approached. The two-thousand-foot-long monstrosity loomed before them. Turrets suggested a close-in-defense system.

"Is this a carrier?" Ted asked.

Char jetted ahead, turned, and slowed. She faced the ship and looked on it as the enemy, her purple eyes cold, like the darkness that enveloped them. Terry eased close beside her.

"What do you see?" he asked. Ted leaned back and forth.

"Closer." Ted pointed toward a nondescript area of the ship.

Char shrugged, her armored suit interpreting the movement as a shoulder twitch. Cory watched the three people she was with and ignored the ship behind her. She didn't care about the ship or who was inside.

Dealing with the enemy had never been her thing.

She reached out a hand, delicately contained within the shipsuit's fabric. She ran one finger down the metal construct of the armor that surrounded her mother's head.

Char glanced at the hand, but her focus was on the ship getting bigger as they floated through open space. Terry whisked away, heading toward where Ted had pointed. Char ensured she had a tight grip on her daughter before activating her jets.

Marcie held on to Sergeant Fitzroy, the recently promoted platoon sergeant. She was taking him under her wing while Kimber was mentoring an older corporal, but not on this mission. The corporal had been left behind in charge of the platoon in case the ship needed them to repel boarders or conduct a follow-on assault.

Contingency on top of contingency. Terry Henry had had to prepare for them all. He planned for flexibility, but without the mechs, the platoon was constrained to operating within a breathable atmosphere. The shipsuits were not designed for combat. One ricochet from a projectile would punch a hole and no matter how enhanced the occupant, they would eventually die without air.

Kelly carried Praeter and remained behind Marcie and Fitzroy. Their target was one of the smaller ships, a destroyer, a tin can, Terry had called it during the briefing. Their mission was to create a diversion. They didn't have the means of hacking into the ship's systems, so they brought a large quantity of explosives.

Same with Kae's team. Unless the aliens surrendered, those two ships were dead.

Marcie turned and activated her jets to slow their approach. Nothing happened.

"Activate the jets!" she yelled within the suit. Nothing happened.

"Hang on," she told Fitzroy. He clenched his jaw and pinched his eyes shut. Marcie braced him within the mech's arms as best she could.

Kelly grabbed Marcie's arm and ran her jets to the maximum. They slowed, but didn't stop. The four warriors slammed into the ship's hull like railgun projectiles.

"Ohh, that hurt," Fitzroy said as he lay on the ship's deck. Artificial gravity within was enough to hold him in place. Marcie's armored legs absorbed the impact for her and she remained crouched. Her boots had dented the ship's surface by almost a finger-length. Kelly had held onto Praeter, who was wincing and stretching his back.

"Thanks for your help," Marcie said, nodding to the other mech. "I'd be really surprised if they didn't know we were here. I expect a repair bot sometime soon, so I think we better move. Maybe they'll decide it was an asteroid."

Kelly looked at the boot-prints in the hull. "Or not." She started walking across the surface toward an area filled with non-geometric shapes. She thought it would be like hiding in a warehouse, and she had no better plan.

Marcie picked up Fitzroy. He yelled into his bubble-helmet, but she couldn't hear him. He'd turned off his comm system. She wondered what was broken, but not for long, because he would heal. The nanocytes in his blood were already at work putting his bones back in place. More importantly than his pain, she had to find cover. Marcie hurried after Kelly, casting glances over her shoulder and toward the stars, looking for any movement of an inbound bot or worse, an alien fighter.

---

Christina blew out a long breath. Unlike the others, she carried Aaron like a backpack. He was draped over her, holding on to the rocket mounts with his legs wrapped around her waist. It gave her the freedom to drive the suit as she needed. In space, one didn't need to be aerodynamic.

Aaron was too tall to fit inside the armor. It was congenial for shorter warriors, but unforgiving beyond a certain height. Kaeden had ordered a custom suit for Aaron, but that was in the backlog, just like the rest of the Bad Company's suits.

Yanmei drove the other mech. She carried Ankh'Po'-Turn like a baby, cradled in her arms. He swiveled his head, more than a human could, to look around. His usual stoic expression was gone as the infinity of the universe weighed on him. He wasn't used to being anyplace that was uncomfortable; he wasn't used to being on the front lines; and he would never get used to being outside the *War Axe* wearing only a shipsuit.

His small hands hurt from gripping Yanmei's armor so tightly.

"Stay frosty, little man," Christina said, nodding toward Ankh. "You need to get us aboard without anyone noticing. Then, we'll punch into the heart of that pig and you work your magic."

Ankh turned his head and looked back into Christina's yellow eyes. He never doubted she was serious.

"I will do my job," he replied noncommittally.

"We know you will, Ankh," Aaron said soothingly.

Christina smiled. An alien and the two weretigers. She couldn't wait to get aboard and show the enemy how weak they were. Whether through stealth or violent action, she would not fail in her mission.

She growled as they approached the massive ship. "What are those doors for?" Aaron asked.

"Those look like hangar bay doors. Lots of hangar bay doors," Ankh whispered.

They drifted in. It went against her nature to hold back, but her training and study of the Force de Guerre and Terry Henry Walton's tactics showed her his reliance on Sun Tzu. Winning a battle without fighting...

That concept stuck in her mind. If they could cripple the ship by taking the computer that drove it, then she would win. Stealth was her best weapon.

As they drifted closer, a light flashed above one of the doors. It rolled up, exposing a hangar with multiple small ships.

Christina and Yanmei touched down gently above the door. They crouched together on the alien ship's hull and waited, helplessly exposed.

# CHAPTER ELEVEN

**The *War Axe***

Captain San Marino put the *War Axe* into a holding position between the fleet of cargo ships and the blockade.

One more cargo ship had departed and none had arrived since Micky last checked. He massaged his temples as he kept his eyes on the main screen.

"Smedley, anything from the alien fleet that might indicate our people have been discovered?"

"There are no indicators. The situation remains status quo. What do you think we would see?" Smedley replied.

"The ships starting to run, or an explosion, or the jammer dropping. Stuff like that."

"There has been no stuff like that."

"Have faith, Skipper," Clifton declared over his shoulder, being one of many who adopted Terry Henry's nickname for the captain. "I think Colonel Walton and his people will deliver fireworks that will let everyone know that you don't fuck with us."

"Clifton! Language." The captain started to wonder who had more influence on his people.

"Oh, shit. Sorry," Clifton muttered, turning back to his controls to calculate a variety of flight profiles for an attack on the blockade.

Just in case.

K'Thrall was doing the same thing, conducting weapon simulations.

"Commander Mac, if the gravitic shields go down again, do you have what you need to get them back up?" Micky asked through the comm system.

"Not in the least," Mac replied. "If our shields go down, we have to run for it before they hit us again."

"Didn't Ted tell you how to fix it?"

"He fixed it with Plato, and he's got Plato with him. And Ted didn't tell me anything. I have no idea why they went down or what it took to bring them back up," Mac admitted.

"I guess I knew that. It looks like our eggs are in one basket. Starspeed, Terry Henry Walton," the captain intoned.

## Alien Ship of the Line #1

Terry rotated and slowed to a perfect two-point landing on the hull. He pushed Ted toward the ship and was relieved to find that he was able to stand without floating away.

"They have artificial gravity technology," Terry said.

Ted ignored him. He didn't have time for stating the obvious. He kneeled beside a panel to one side of the round hatch, studying the interface for a moment before pulling a handle below it. The group watched expectantly, disappointed when nothing immediately happened. Ted placed his gloved hand on the structure between the pad and the hatch. He nodded slowly.

Terry took a deep breath, stopping the instant the hatch started to retract sideways, rolling into a space between the external hull and the interior framework. The ship was double-hulled, a standard practice for Earth's surface fleets to increase survivability.

"Some lessons are universal," Terry said as he climbed into a large airlock. Ted pulled himself inside and Char pushed Cory ahead before bringing up the rear. Once inside, Ted tapped at the panel beside the hatch that led inside the ship.

"Green and red?" Terry whispered as he looked at the panel. The symbols on it showed everything. He did not have to understand the alien's language.

As TH liked to say, it was idiot simple. The interior hatch contained a porthole-sized window through which Terry glanced. Beyond was a standard corridor, empty. Terry grinned behind his suit's helmet. When the hatch opened, he found that he was barely able to squeeze through after Ted who took a sharp right and started to run.

"Ted, get the fuck back here!" Terry tried to tiptoe down the corridor, but the mech wasn't built for silence.

Char hesitated, torn between getting out of the mech and going after Terry and Ted. Cory bolted from the airlock to follow the other two. Char didn't want to lose them, so she squeezed into the corridor and crouched as she ran after the others.

The two mechs pounded the deck like a pile driver being run by a steamroller.

Terry caught up to Ted and grabbed his collar. Ted struggled, but Terry was having none of it. He locked the grip and picked him up. TH stalked to a side hatch. He stopped and listened, using his suit's enhanced capabilities. When he heard nothing, he opened the hatch and shoved Ted through. He crawled into the storage space behind him. Cory entered, then Char moved in and shut the hatch behind her.

The colonel moved to the side, locked his suit down, and climbed out the back. He took a deep breath of the ship's air, knowing that the suit had declared it to be normal air, slightly higher in oxygen than what they were used to.

"Ted, goddammit! Where in the fuck were you going? You put this whole mission at risk making us run down the corridor in our suits." Terry clenched his teeth. A vein stood out on his forehead. He reached out and grabbed Ted, picking him up and then slamming his feet back into the deck. Terry breathed out heavily before letting go of the werewolf.

"Plato sensed the power of their AI. We must go there," Ted declared as he pulled his hood back. His gloves retracted automatically into the shipsuit's sleeves. Ted watched the suit transform itself back into normal attire, fascinated by the utility.

"We go together, and it'll be best if we don't announce

that we're here. Let's give it a few minutes before we strike out again."

Char moved to the side of the hatch, parked her suit, and got out. She shook her head, sending her hair cascading over her shoulders. Terry watched, distracted for a moment.

Cory removed her hood and without thinking, brushed her hair to cover her wolf ears. She held her breath for an inordinate amount of time before taking in the ship's air.

"The air's fine," Char offered.

"I don't know. Something doesn't seem right about this place."

"You got that right. What's wrong is that it feels like the *War Axe*, a human ship, not just a ship with some stolen human technology," Terry suggested.

Char looked to the round activator in the center of the hatch. "This looks like it's from a United States warship." Char pointed. She spun the wheel and dogged the hatch.

"We need to get to the ship's AI," Ted declared. He held the black box containing Plato.

"I can't believe you brought your AI." Char shook her head before closing her eyes to explore the Etheric, find where the warm bodies were as well as get insight into the ship's layout.

"There are few people on board, and no one in this area," she said, rolling her monologue as she followed the other dimension through the ship. "This is a carrier, with fighters and transport ships, although I think the ships are all flown by computers. There doesn't seem to be a place for an entity, human or otherwise. Wait! Here comes four people, human or human hybrid. They're heading for the airlock.

"They've reached the airlock. There is some confusion. They are looking at the deck. Now they're coming back this way."

Terry growled, rolling his shoulders and checking the Jean Dukes Special that had been wedged against his side while he was in the suit. He rocked slightly as he prepared for the expected fight. "On my order, pull the hatch open if they cycle the action," Terry told Cory. He stood to the side where it would open. Char put a hand on his shoulder and leaned in behind him.

Ted pushed Plato into Cory's hands before pulling his shipsuit off and changing into a werewolf. He stood on all fours behind Terry and Char. Together, they waited as the four crew of the enemy ship approached, stopped at the hatch, and reached for the wheel.

## Alien Ship of the Line #2

Two small fighter spacecraft maneuvered from the opening before accelerating into the darkness. The door started to roll back down.

"Is that our way in?" Christina asked. Without waiting for an answer, she leapt over the edge and used her suit's jets to angle down the side. She peeked into the bay, looking for any living creatures. Her recce of the hangar bay said it was empty.

Yanmei followed her down, staying on the side away from the door.

With a nod and a wave, the two suited warriors walked

through the door and dove to the side, depositing their passengers as they stood still and waited. Their suits gave them an enhanced view of the hangar bay, better than what their own Were eyes provided.

There were no more spacecraft within. The bay was large enough to hold two fighters and the support equipment for them.

When the door closed all the way, the lights within the hangar extinguished, leaving Christina and her team completely in the dark.

"Got any ideas?" Aaron asked. Christina and Yanmei both shook their heads, but no one saw.

"I think we should turn on the lights and go find what we're here to find," Ankh said flatly.

As Christina was looking to turn on the suit's exterior lights, a hatch opened to the hangar bay and a person walked through. The lights came up to a twilight level. The individual walked halfway across the bay, picked up a tool-box, turned, and walked back to the hatch, closing it behind him. The lights dimmed and then extinguished.

"Sure looked like a human," Yanmei whispered.

"Does that change anything?" Christina asked.

*No,* Aaron answered using his comm chip. *It means that we know how evil they can be without having to guess. The worst creatures in the universe are human, as are the best. Figuring out where this group stands will determine if we have to destroy it or not. Maybe we can talk the crew out of the blockade.*

*Interesting,* Christina replied. *The suit says we have an oxygen-nitrogen atmosphere. Let's park them out of sight and go take a look-see.*

Christina turned on her suit's lights, high beams from

each shoulder that illuminated what was in front of her. She turned slowly from one side to the other.

Yanmei activated her lights. Farther to her right was an area with crates and boxes. She headed that way with Ankh in tow. She clambered behind a pile, shut down her suit, and climbed out. Christina watched, providing cover as Yanmei transitioned.

The weretiger pulled the oversized railgun from the mech suit's shoulder and hoisted it in her arms. Ankh moved from behind the crates and walked toward the hatch still illuminated by Christina's suit.

She waited until the Crenellian and Aaron were in place before she turned off her suit's lights, plunging the small hangar bay back into darkness.

Clearing the crates by touch alone, she squinted in the direction of the door, letting her yellow Pricolici eyes take in the light. She saw the shapes of her team. She walked boldly across the open area, tripping over a tie-down point as she walked. She heard Aaron snicker.

"Yeah, yeah, I get it. When I'm sitting in the captain's chair of this pig, you'll be down here removing that tripping hazard."

"Yes, ma'am," Aaron mumbled. Christina joined them at the hatch.

"I don't hear anything from the other side," Yanmei offered.

Christina listened, then whispered, "When that guy opened the hatch, did anyone see what was beyond?"

"A nondescript corridor," Aaron said. "That's all I saw."

"I'll go first," Christina said. She gripped the hatch handle, and stopped. "Which way do we go, Ankh?"

The Crenellian looked up at her. His big, bald head clear in the nearly total darkness of the hangar bay. "I have no idea."

"I was worried you were going to say that. Eenie, meenie, miney, mo…" Christina took a deep breath. "We go right. Be ready."

She opened the hatch and stuck her head out, looking left and then quickly to the right. She froze when she saw two faces look back at her from a meter away.

## Alien Destroyer #1

Marcie and Kelly stood perfectly still as they leaned against an outcropping on the smaller ship. Fitzroy and Praeter hung onto the mechs, trying to remain still. The four willed themselves to be invisible.

Electronically they were, but they stood out, should anyone look at that part of the ship.

"What do we do now?" Fitzroy grunted as the nanocytes continued to repair his leg.

"We wait," Marcie said impatiently. She fidgeted within her suit, but none of the movements manifested themselves externally. Her suit remained perfectly still as she imagined she was nothing but a black hole, from which no light would escape.

Kelly shook her head and settled in to wait. Praeter checked the air in his shipsuit. He had some time before things became grim.

CHAPTER TWELVE

**Alien Battleship #1**

Joseph and Kim walked slowly across the ship's outer hull. Weapons turrets bristled all around them as they continued toward the circle of light that Joseph assumed was an airlock.

The light went out and Joseph froze.

"What the hell?" Kim muttered. Bundin paid no attention to the loss of light. He strolled across the outside of the battleship as if he owned it.

*What's your hurry?* Joseph asked.

*Can't hold my breath much longer,* Bundin replied.

*Oh, crap!* Joseph berated himself for not realizing his friend's limitation.

Bundin reached the hatch and looked at it, but his tentacles were ill-suited for work beneath his feet. He stood aside and waited. Joseph hurried up, then he and Petricia studied the panel beside the hatch. The picture showing to pull the lever was all they needed. Joseph took hold and gently pulled the lever. Kim joined them, unhappy that Joseph had pulled the access before she arrived.

She moved to the opposite side of the hatch and looked in, her railgun at the ready. Auburn cringed, not wanting to be next to the weapon if Kim had to unleash its power. Bundin walked toward the hatch and went inside. The others followed. Even with two mechs, a Podder, and two people, there was plenty of room.

Auburn pushed off Kimber, dropping to the deck immediately. He walked to the interior hatch and looked through the small window at an empty corridor.

He turned to the others and shook his head, then looked back through the window, hoping that the space beyond would remain empty. The atmosphere within the chamber did not change.

"Punch the button beside the door," Kimber suggested. Auburn looked at it. There was a green light with an image of the inside hatch. There was a red light next to a picture of the external hatch. Auburn pressed the green button, which initiated the exchange. The sound of air rushing into the chamber came through clearly.

The button flashed green until it turned a solid green. Auburn tried to activate the hatch, and it opened with ease. He looked into the corridor before stepping through. Bundin's mouth opened and he inhaled deeply. He wheezed and coughed before settling in to breathing normally.

"The air is fine," he said softly.

He ambled through the hatch. Petricia followed, with the two mechs close behind. Auburn turned left. No one had a better idea, so they continued in that direction. At the first corner, Auburn ran head-first into a crewman.

"Watch out!" the man called, before stepping back in shock.

Auburn smiled broadly, his white teeth gleaming behind his dark skin. "Hi, there," he said in his deep voice. He waved his hand behind him, signaling for the others to stop before they were seen.

"Who are you?" the man asked, slowly pulling a wrench from a small tool bag he was carrying. Auburn had a railgun in a combat sling over his shoulder, but had no intention of pulling the barrel upward to threaten the man.

Bundin turned the corner and bumped into Auburn's back.

"What the hell is that thing?" the man shouted, before changing to a high-pitched scream. "EMERGENCY!"

Warning klaxons started blaring and red lights flashed. He threw his wrench at Auburn, who easily ducked it. The man turned to run, but Auburn was enhanced and a trained warrior. He caught the man in two steps and slung him sideways into the wall. Auburn pulled the man's arm up behind him and redirected him back toward the others.

Petricia removed a pair of zip ties from a zippered pouch on the outside of her leg. They tied his hands behind his back, then his legs, and finished by zipping his hands to his ankles. Kim carried him like a suitcase until she deposited him into the airlock chamber. She closed the hatch as they went the opposite direction from where they were headed before.

The klaxons continued while the lights flashed.

"We need to find cover and ditch these suits," Kimber said as they started to run down the empty corridor.

## Alien Battleship #2

Timmons held Sue tightly as he walked carefully down the outside hull of the alien spaceship that they had designated a battleship. It sported numerous gun turrets on its bulk.

Shonna teetered as the ship lurched beneath her.

Timmons stopped and crouched. The battleship began to move, slowly at first, but it quickly picked up speed. The artificial gravity within the ship helped, but they were still on the outside of a moving starship. What if it sailed out of the system? What if it gated? Could they survive being outside as the ship passed over the event horizon?

Questions flashed through the engineers' minds as the ship moved out of the blockade and started running from one of the string of ships to the other. It banked and began a long arc as it turned toward the flashes of light that were the cargo fleet parked at the edge of the heliosphere.

"Well now," Shonna started. "Ain't this a shit sandwich."

"Deep-fried with extra shit," Merrit replied.

"We need to get inside, maybe stop this pig before it goes into battle with the good guys. That's our new mission. No one will know if this thing gets destroyed from the inside or the outside as it closes with the *War Axe*. We have to make sure that it's dead before the *Axe* kills it."

"And us," Sue added needlessly.

Timmons stepped carefully forward, making sure to

always have one boot locked onto the hull before moving the other. "There," he said, pointing.

Shonna didn't reply, keeping her focus on walking across the battleship as it accelerated toward the stars.

## Alien Destroyer #2

Kae spotted the airlock as they approached. He guided them in to where they landed beside the hatch. He kneeled down, studied the panel for five seconds, then pulled the handle. Capples and Gomez watched.

"That's it?" Capples wondered aloud.

"The more evolved a species becomes, the more likely their instructions will be easy to follow," Kae replied philosophically.

"Or they are used to dealing with knuckle-draggers like us," Capples said, watching the hatch and smiling as it started to retract into the hull. The light within came on and he jumped through, landing softly. He put Gomez down and waited for Kaeden.

Kae caught movement out of the corner of his eye. His instincts kicked in and he brought his railgun up to fire, stopping himself when he saw the battleship accelerate past and turn away from the blockade on a vector toward the *War Axe*.

"Was that the pack's target?" Kae asked.

"I believe so," Ramses answered. "Sonofabitch."

"I hope they made it inside." Kae turned his attention back to entering the enemy ship. He pushed Ramses through and followed him in.

Capples punched the green button, closing the exterior

hatch and pumping atmosphere into the space. When the light turned solid green, the interior hatch popped. Capples counted down using his fingers. On one, he pulled the door inward and jumped through, with Gomez diving to the right as Cap dove left.

The corridor was empty. Ramses walked through and stopped, trying to decide which way would be best. He shrugged and held his hands up. Kae ducked as he went through the hatch. Using the suit's systems, he determined that the hotter section of the tin can was toward the rear. Their mission, just like Marcie's, was to create a diversion. Nothing like blowing the engines to get everyone's attention.

"Aft, my good man." Kae pointed to the right. Gomez took the lead with Kae close behind. Ramses followed while Cap brought up the rear. Gomez and Ramses pulled their hoods back and sucked in lungs full of the ship air. Kae and Cap remained in their suits.

The shipsuits started automatically refilling each suit's air supply.

They had no intention of leaving their armored suits behind as long as they could fit inside the corridors and were able to get through hatches.

"Peace through superior firepower," Kae said softly.

## Alien Ship of the Line #2

Christina looked at the two human men as they stared back at her suit's helmet. She launched through the opening and reached out in a lightning quick movement, grabbing both men by their necks. They grabbed her wrists and struggled, but neither was able to sound the alarm. Aaron hurried around her and pulled his zip ties.

The men continued to struggle.

"Humans?" she asked.

The men stopped at the sound of the human tongue coming through the suit's speakers.

"Who are you?" one managed to ask.

"Christina. Who are you?" she replied, releasing some of the pressure on his throat as the others surrounded them.

"I'm Twee-a-Dil," he replied without further elaboration.

"Nice to meet you, Twee. And you, what's your name?" Christina pressed. She let go of the first man as Aaron pulled his arms back and secured the zip tie. Yanmei gripped him by the arm as Aaron secured the second man's arms. Christina stepped back. "I asked you a question."

"I am For-a-Doo."

She wanted to make fun of the names, but thought better of it. "We need to find the computer mainframe. You will take us there."

"Like hell I will!" the first man retorted. Christina didn't remember telling her hand to slap the man, but an instant later, she saw him lying on the ground. Aaron looked questioningly at her before hauling the man back to his feet.

"You had best watch your mouth," Aaron advised while shaking his head in Christina's direction.

"We don't need your help. We'll get there by ourselves." Christina turned to head left down the corridor. She activated her rear cameras to watch their expressions. The quick look of relief told her what she wanted to know.

She turned back and pointed over their heads. "It's that way."

"What do we do with these two?" Aaron asked.

"We'll dump the suits in the airlock and take these fine gentlemen with us."

Aaron and Ankh remained in the corridor with the men while Christina and Yanmei returned to the airlock. They parked the suits where they wouldn't be readily seen through the small window and climbed out.

They returned to the corridor and the men's breath caught as they saw the striking women.

"Give it a rest or I will beat you senseless," Christina snarled.

The two men could not tear their eyes away from the women. Everyone grew uncomfortable. "Come on, you two. Let's find us a mainframe so we can say, 'hi!'," Aaron told them, bodily dragging them around in a circle and pushing them down the corridor.

"What are you?" the second man asked after being forced to look away from the women.

"I'm a Crenellian. My name is Ankh'Po'Turn," he said proudly, tipping his chin back to look up at the much taller human. "Why the strange reaction to the females? You act as if you have not seen one before."

"We haven't," the man admitted, trying to turn around, but Aaron kept them looking forward. "Very few get selected for breeding on our planet. The others serve in the fleet."

"Stop!" Christina called from the rear. She walked around to get in front of the men. "The second-class citizens have to serve in the military? And the non-military are the ones who get to have children?"

The men nodded while looking at her with wide eyes.

"That's fucked up thirty-seven different ways from Sunday. You come from a fucked-up culture, which is probably why you are so fucked up."

"Not everyone reveres women as we do. Some of the soldiers despise them, thinking them too elitist. No women serve in the fleet. They remain on the home world living in pampered luxury."

"So the men chosen to breed worship at the altar of Princess Love Chunks?" Christina mocked. "Or they carry fire and brimstone to purge the evil that is women. Is there no middle ground?"

The men still stared wide-eyed.

"That's enough, you're starting to creep me out," Aaron told them. "Let's go. Onward we venture to the mainframe!"

"To the mainframe," Ankh repeated. He struck out ahead of the men. Christina stepped back to allow Aaron to push them forward, keeping one hand on each of their heads to keep them from turning around.

"Who's Princess Love Chunks? Would your mother approve of your snark?" Aaron whispered over his shoulder.

"TH is a bad influence, I tell you. No, my mother would slap those words right out of my mouth. I better be careful when I go home for a visit."

One of the men managed to turn around and look wistfully at Christina. Aaron squeezed the man's neck until he turned back.

Yanmei raised one eyebrow as she made eye contact with Christina. "That was weird," Yanmei whispered with her slight Chinese accent.

"I'll second that, sister," Christina agreed.

## Alien Destroyer #1

"My patience is at the breaking point," Marcie complained. Fitzroy nodded slowly as he tried to control his breathing and use less oxygen.

"Time to find a way in?" Kelly asked.

"I think it's time. I wonder how the others are doing." Marcie picked up the sergeant and slowly walked onto the open hull of the tin can. Her head ratcheted back and forth as she looked for any movement, any hint that they'd been spotted.

She wasn't sure what that would look like, but she expected it would include some kind of gunfire, whether railguns or plasma rounds or other alien weapons of war.

*Bathe the shell in fire to cleanse the impurities,* she thought. *Might as well go out loud and proud.*

Marcie picked up her pace, striding boldly across the open hull, past a weapons turret and a railgun mount. Standard weaponry. She used the suit's enhanced sensors to look more closely at the ship's construction. Welds. Metal that didn't look exotic. It dented, as she remembered too clearly. Protrusions with wires, boxes, and handholds.

"You notice anything peculiar about this ship?" Marcie asked.

Fitzroy had been studying it, too. "It's odd in how familiar it is. They're not very alien, for being aliens."

"My thoughts exactly, Fitz. It's different from what's in the Federation fleet, but it's the same, too."

"Up ahead," Kelly said, brushing past Marcie and Fitzroy. "I think I see a hatch set into the hull."

Just like the others, they saw the panel with the graphic and the handle. Kelly pulled on it and activated the airlock's outer hatch. It retracted into the hull and they climbed in. As if they had planned for it to be that easy.

Marcie had hoped, but she carried explosives, too. She knew that she would get into that ship and didn't care if they knew she was coming.

Only Ted had been confident that it would be easy to get into the ships. He understood that they had not been designed to repel individual boarders.

He had no idea what they would find inside, but he wasn't concerned about that. He counted on the others to protect him while he did what he needed to do. For Marcie, the real work was about to begin.

# CHAPTER THIRTEEN

**Alien Ship of the Line #1**

As soon as the storeroom hatch started to open, Cory yanked on it, ripping it from the crewmember's hands. Terry and Char rushed into the corridor followed by a shaggy gray werewolf.

Terry pulled his punch because the men were unarmed, holding his fist a hair from the man's shocked face. He reached around and put him into a one-armed headlock instead. The others stumbled backward when they saw the purple-eyed Char bear down on them.

When the man in the back fell, the other two tripped over him and went down. The three lay in a jumble as Ted growled at them.

"We didn't know!" one of those in the man-pile declared.

"Didn't know what?" Char asked.

"That a woman was on board."

Terry let the man out of the headlock and pinned him

against the bulkhead with one arm. Cory walked into the corridor.

"Two of them!" another exclaimed.

"I don't think they get out much," Terry suggested before turning his attention back to the men. "Although we're more than happy to agree that the striking beauty of these two is incomparable, we don't have time for such a distraction. We need to get to your ship's AI. And that needs to happen sooner rather than later, if you get my drift. I also notice that you seem completely unintimidated by a werewolf. Do you have them where you come from?"

"We have dogs. They are our best friend. This one is probably hungry. He looks skinny. A good meal and he'll settle down," the man explained matter-of-factly.

"You've lost your mojo, Ted. I think Felicity will enjoy this story. Might as well get dressed," Char said. Ted harrumphed as much as a werewolf could, then trotted through the storeroom hatch.

Terry watched him go, before asking the serious questions. With little prompting, the men explained what Christina and Yanmei had learned on the other ship.

Char finally decided to let the men stand. They bunched together as they paid rapt attention to Char and Cory. Terry stood between the men and his family to pull their attention away.

Ted appeared in his shipsuit carrying the box with the AI's consciousness. The crewmen didn't notice.

"You're human," Terry stated as he looked from one face to the next. "Where do you come from?"

"The home world," one man willingly offered.

"Coordinates or a name, maybe?"

The men shook their heads as they craned their necks to get a better look at the women. Char waggled her fingers at them over Terry's shoulder. The men smiled in return.

"Stop it," Terry said out the side of his mouth.

"I wonder what it's like to maintain a harem," Char said.

"Have we been chosen for breeding?" one man asked hopefully.

Terry coughed and snorted.

"No. No breeding. They both have mates and none of that matters. We need to get to your AI. You can help us, or you get zip-tied and stuffed in a closet. Your choice. You have three seconds to decide. Three. Two. One. Zip tie it is," Terry said, never giving the men a chance to answer.

He pushed them toward the opening. Ted inched away. Plato knew where the AI was.

Cory made each man turn around so she could secure their hands. One by one, they entered the storeroom. Terry followed them in to cuff their feet and then link their hands to their feet.

"Oww!" one of the men complained.

"Stop your whining. You could have a punched face, but instead, you get zipped up. Relax, it'll be easier on your joints. You'll be freed soon enough," Terry told them before returning to the corridor. He paused to lean his head back in before shutting the hatch. "Bye, bye, now. Miss you already."

He cycled the hatch, securing it.

"Really?" Char said as they hustled after Ted, whose patience had run out.

"Sorry about that," Terry apologized. "We're on an alien

ship that's not alien at all, crewed by human males who aren't allowed to see women in person. I'm not sure this could be any more fucked up, but they don't seem to know how to fight, and they're unarmed, so our chances of surviving this have improved a whole lot. I hope the others are finding the same thing."

They jogged through empty corridors behind Ted, who was communing with his AI through some means that Terry and Char didn't know about. Cory kept pace, staying close to Ted to keep him from running headlong into trouble.

"We have women with each team except for Kaeden's..." Char let the thought drift.

Terry wondered whether that was good or bad.

### The *War Axe*

"All hands, battle stations. I say again, all hands to battle stations," the captain said over the ship-wide broadcast. He could feel the energy of the crew.

Not in any direct way, but he knew how they were responding, hurrying to their damage control stations, checking systems, and battening down the hatches.

"The tactical team led by Timmons was supposed to board that particular vessel," Smedley reported.

Micky watched the icon grow larger as it held its course. "Maybe they've been compromised or somehow never made it aboard," he reasoned.

When Smedley showed green, he dropped the final bulkheads, sealing sections of the ship to maximize the survivability of both ship and crew.

"Bringing the mains to bear," K'Thrall reported.

"Wait for my command," Micky ordered. The bridge crew fidgeted as the alien battleship accelerated toward them. "Smedley, what is the optimal firing range?"

"Within the range of the EMP weapon," Smedley answered the unasked question.

"And if we fire before they enter the optimal envelope?"

"Our chances of hitting the target are reduced by up to ninety percent."

"Thank you, Smedley. K'Thrall, prepare to fire warning shots in a pattern in front of the enemy ship. Slow fire to warn them off," the captain ordered.

"Offset angle of one degree to approach, rate of fire is two plasma charges per second. Ready to fire."

"Fire," Micky said calmly.

## Alien Battleship #2

The light reached them before the plasma round. Timmons watched helplessly as the undulating mass rolled toward them. He stopped and braced himself.

"We need to keep moving," Sue said softly.

Timmons realized the futility of his effort. He gritted his teeth and returned to plodding forward.

The first round skipped past the battleship, then the next and the next. Timmons expected that the *War Axe* would walk the plasma into the alien ship, but instead it was creating a barrier between the alien spaceship and the cargo fleet.

The battleship started to slowly turn away, beginning a new arc. Timmons breathed a sigh of relief as he carefully forced his way ahead, one magnetic boot after the other.

Merrit had wrapped himself around Shonna's front, letting the ship's motion pin him to his mate, while she pulled herself forward along an invisible line from aft to stern.

Timmons couldn't turn, he could only cycle his cameras back and forth. He felt like he was within a hurricane, even though there was no resistance in space. The ship threatened to fly out from beneath him at any moment. He wondered if he would be able to fly back to the *War Axe* if he let go.

But they hadn't accomplished their mission and the alpha was counting on the werewolves to take care of the battleship. He put the thoughts of jumping out of his mind and searched for the way inside. There had to be a hatch somewhere.

### Alien Battleship #1

The klaxons and flashing red lights helped hurry Joseph's pace. Having removed their suits in one of many empty spaces that lined the corridor, they were free to breathe the alien air. Free to move without the clump-clump of the armored boots on the deck.

Joseph reached out with his mind to touch other minds in the area. Now that he knew they were human, it made it easier. The initial contact with the Podder had been difficult, but at least the creature had been subdued. He refused to contact alien minds that were free to retaliate.

Joseph knew his way around human minds.

Petricia held his arm as they walked. She knew where his mind had gone and in times like those, she protected him. Theirs was a partnership of souls. Sometimes, they didn't need to speak. They just *knew*.

Bundin ambled down the corridor, seemingly immune to the emergency condition within the ship. Auburn was behind the Podder and Kim assumed the role of tail end Charlie. She had her Jean Dukes Special out and walked backward, watching the team's six o'clock. She dialed it up from the lowest setting to number two.

She wasn't taking any chances.

Joseph stopped and reached out to steady himself against the wall. Bundin almost ran into him. Petricia's brow furled in concern.

"They are human, but different. They don't think like we do as they were raised on an alien world with alien masters. There is a consciousness on board that is unlike anything I've ever seen, but we are new out here. Maybe this is common. I don't know," Joseph said softly.

"Bundin?" Petricia asked.

"I can't answer Joseph's concerns. Aren't we here to find the intelligence within? Find that which drives these ships and remove their ability to cause further harm to the people of Alchon Prime?"

Before anyone could answer, Joseph motioned toward a door. "In there, quick!"

They hurried through, as much as they could with an over-sized creature like Bundin. Kim pushed the door shut, although she wanted to see what was coming. She didn't cycle the lock. She held it just in case she needed to throw it open and race into the fray. Joseph held a finger to his lips.

Kim stroked the side of her JDS. She had yet to fire it. Immediately after her dad had given it to her, they boarded the *War Axe* and left on this mission. That was three days ago.

The people of Alchon Prime were starving.

Her lip curled in a sneer. If she had to start killing people, she was ready. If she had to blow the ship, she was ready for that, too. As Colonel Terry Henry Walton preached: No one was more important than the mission, so the leader's job was make sure that the mission was worth dying for.

She slowly opened the hatch even though Joseph was shaking his head. She peered out, seeing no one. She opened it further, leading with the barrel of her pistol as she looked over the top of it.

Walking away from her were two men wearing workers' coveralls. They appeared to be talking like friends, while ignoring the emergency klaxons and flashing lights. They continued on their way until turning a corner farther down the corridor.

Kim assumed a firing position to the right of the door while the others left the space and resumed heading in their original direction.

"Are we going in the right direction?" Auburn asked.

"I think so," Joseph said, stumbling as he tried to touch the crews' minds to give the team a warning.

"How many crew on board?" Auburn asked, always

thinking logistically. Kimber heard the question and wondered why she hadn't asked it. For this mission, Joseph was the team leader, but she was still a major and well-trained in tactics. She cursed herself for not taking a more active role. Joseph did not think tactically. He reacted.

He needed her for the tactical execution of the mission. More importantly, she needed to be there for him.

"Maybe one hundred," Joseph muttered as he worked to find the minds throughout the ship.

"On a ship this size? Only one hundred?" Kim couldn't believe it. "Are they scattered? No big concentration of them? As long as we know, we can easily deal with either."

"Scattered. No more than four in any one place."

"What are we waiting for? It's time to find that intelligence and introduce ourselves."

Joseph and Petricia led the way with Bundin following close behind.

"Keep an eye on Joseph. Don't let that alien consciousness, or whatever the hell he called it, get to him," Kim implored her husband.

Auburn nodded to his wife.

She winked at him before resuming walking backward, watching for anyone approaching from behind.

Kimber expected the challenge for control of the battleship would come from something other than the human crew.

## Alien Destroyer #2

Kaeden marched toward the rear of the tin can with

grim determination on his face. He had no idea how the others were doing.

For his part of the mission, it didn't matter. Create a diversion, and if he could take the destroyer out of the fight at the same time, that was his idea of a win-win.

A human face appeared in the corridor before them.

"Hey!" Gomez called out. The man started to run. "Don't run. We're your friends!"

The man pulled at the air as he tried to run faster.

No one had a stun gun, but Gomez had his knife. He pulled it and threw in a single motion, adding a little extra twist. The butt of the knife hit the man in the back of the head. He careened into a wall, stumbled, and fell. Gomez ran after him.

The warrior picked up his knife and put it back in its sheath before lifting the man to his feet. His eyes rolled around in his head as he tottered.

"Sorry about that, boss. I think I hit him a little harder than I meant. Don't know my own strength."

Kae shook his head. They all knew how strong they were. They'd been practicing with their enhancements for a couple months.

"Sure," Kae replied evenly. "Truss him up and dump him so we can keep moving."

Gomez made short work of the man, tossing him into an empty room.

"Check these other spaces," Kae ordered, nodding to Capples and Ramses.

They started pulling open the hatches, using the two-person methodology for room clearing with one person opening the door and the second heading in, looking over the barrel of his railgun.

"Empty?" Kae said knowingly.

"All empty," Cap reported.

Kae waved them off, checking more of the spaces. His suit's microphones were picking up the hum of machinery.

"Let's go make some noise," Kae said in a low voice, leading the way toward the sound.

Two of the human crew appeared in the corridor. He motioned for them to go away and they ran.

"What's up, boss?" Capples asked using the suit's internal comm system.

"Those guys are nothing. They aren't armed. They aren't dangerous. And the closer we get to the engines, the shorter their life expectancy gets, so we might as well let them hide in fear," Kaeden replied.

"Makes sense," Cap answered. Ramses and Gomez had their railguns ready as they jogged to keep up with Kaeden's mech.

The corridor ended with a large hatch to their left, toward the interior of the ship. Kae put his hand on the door, feeling the power within. Not a vibration, as starship engines didn't rotate like physical propulsion systems.

Kae's armored hand gripped the circular wheel in the middle and spun it. He pushed the hatch inward and plowed through the opening, bringing his railgun to bear in one smooth motion.

He froze when he saw what was before him. Gomez and Ramses squeezed past, stopping at Kae's side. Cap was blocked in the corridor.

The human crew were lined up between the mechs and a metal bank with blue flashing lights that raced from one end to the other, then started over again, giving the impression of forward movement. There was other equipment in the space, but the men stood, arms stretched out, holding hands.

"So you are willing to make a stand," Kaeden said coldly. "But standing between us and the people of Alchon Prime will not make your sacrifice any less worthless. You had the chance to remove your blockade, now you're making us do it. So there you are."

Kaeden picked a spot on the equipment and prepared to fire.

"You might not want to be here for this," he told the two men in shipsuits. "Meet us at the airlock."

Gomez and Ramses backed into the corridor and started to run.

"Make some room," Cap requested.

"Stay out there, just in case blowing this thing turns out badly." Kaeden started to laugh. His life had been long, but he wasn't ready to end it. "Maybe it's better if we just blow it remotely?"

"I like that idea," Capples replied, nodding his helmeted head. "You know how much they need us."

Kae reached over his back and pulled the shaped explosives from the thin pack. He looked at the two shaped charges, verified that the suit could communicate with them, and then turned back to the alien technology.

"I'd love to know more about this stuff, but that's not my mission. Sorry, gentlemen. Time to pack it in. If you have lifeboats, I suggest you go find a spot and launch yourselves into space. Standoff distance is a great survival concept," Kaeden suggested.

"Now that you have your human bravado out of the way, let's talk," a disembodied voice said, filling the space around them.

# CHAPTER FOURTEEN

**Alien Battleship #2**

Timmons bent over ninety degrees to better see the panel. He reached down and pulled the lever, disappointed that nothing happened.

Shonna and Merrit caught up with him and watched. Even with the armored suits, the effort of walking along the hull of a speeding starship was extreme.

The hatch popped and retracted slowly into the hull. Timmons pushed Sue inside the space, using his body as a backstop until he could follow her in. Shonna followed suit. When the four were inside, Sue tapped the green light on the panel and the external hatch secured, atmosphere was pumped in, and the interior hatch popped.

By the time the door opened, both Timmons and Shonna had already climbed out of their armor. They breathed heavily. Both had sweat running down their heads.

Sue pulled the hatch toward her and walked into the

corridor beyond. Timmons jumped out after her, looking left and right.

"Please be more careful!" he cautioned.

"While you were *disrobing*, I took a quick walk within the Etheric, looking for anyone pulling energy from it. I knew there was nothing out here or anywhere close," she replied with a half-smile. He rubbed her shoulder.

"Sorry. I'm still on edge after that little bit where I thought the *War Axe* was going to kill us. That would not have been our finest moment." Timmons went pale, briefly, as he thought about how close he'd come to dying. There had been a few occasions in the past one hundred and fifty years, but this was foremost in his mind.

Clinging to the outside of the alien battleship and watching a string of plasma rounds approach. The helplessness he felt. Maybe someone else would have seen beauty in the stars. Timmons only saw death by fire in the cold and dark of space with his mate in his arms, unable to touch her one last time.

He shivered and looked away. Sue had been with him for a long time.

She knew. None of the seemingly immortal took brushes with death well.

Timmons snarled, forcing himself to be angry so he could focus. Terry had taught him that trick. The werewolf clenched his fists, digging his fingernails into his palms.

He brought the oversized railgun up and pointed it down the corridor. He took one step, then hesitated. Sue shook her head.

"I don't know which way," she said softly.

Timmons gritted his teeth. "Then it doesn't matter

which way we go. Let's find the brains of this outfit and give it a lobotomy."

He turned around and headed forward, for absolutely no reason at all besides the fact that he was angry.


### The *War Axe*

"The alien vessel has veered away from an attack vector," Smedley reported.

Micky was hunched over, his stomach muscles protesting the strain. He grunted when he tried to turn his head. The captain closed his eyes and rolled his head back and forth, trying to will away the stress of the encounter.

"Was there any electronic probing or attack that we didn't sense? Are there drones or bodies floating toward us through space?"

"The gravitic shields are active," K'Thrall said, poking his head out from within the holo screens. "Should they impact our shields, they will have a very bad day."

Micky looked askance at the Yollin.

"Then it's settled." Micky tapped the controls on the arm of the captain's chair. "Stand down from general quarters. Resume normal ship operations," he ordered over the ship-wide broadcast.

Clifton slid his hood back and blinked rapidly as the fresh air attacked his eyes. He looked to the captain. "Remain in position?" he asked. "Or are we going to go after him, make an example of that Fuckbert?"

Micky put his forehead in one hand and massaged his temples with his thumb and middle finger.

"We're not going to attack the aliens. Let the colonel conduct his mission. I have faith that he'll get the job done."

Clifton watched the alien battleship arc away from the *War Axe* and toward the blockade of ships. "I wonder if Timmons and his team are okay."

"I wish we knew about all of them," Micky whispered to himself.

### Alien Ship of the Line #1

Ted turned at a T-intersection and headed toward the interior of the ship.

"Time to kick ass and chew bubblegum?" Terry asked Char as they jogged after Ted. Cory stayed close, having no intention of getting left behind. She shook her head, never understanding her father's inclination toward inane banter when they were in the middle of a high-stress situation.

"Fresh out of bubblegum," Char answered.

Ted slowed to a walk. A man appeared in the corridor. Ted didn't appear to notice him as he walked past. Char expected an extreme reaction.

"BLASPHEMER!" the man howled when he caught sight of Char. She smiled as she made a beeline for him. He lunged forward.

Clumsily. She slapped his hands and backhanded his nose. His head snapped back and bounced once off the wall before he stumbled forward. Char rotated at the waist, smacking her right fist into the palm of her left hand to solidify the elbow strike that caught the man in the temple.

He went down like a sack of bricks.

"Blaspheme that," she told him, stepping around his unconscious form to continue after Ted.

Terry glanced back and motioned for Cory to catch up to Char. He waited until the women were ahead before searching the man for a badge or any device. He was disappointed when he didn't find anything, although it had been expected. A theory was forming within his mind, but it remained ethereal.

It needed to gel more before he could articulate what he was feeling.

He jumped up and ran when he realized that the others had turned a corner and were no longer in sight.

Terry raced around the turn and dodged to avoid running over his daughter. He bounced off the wall and slid to a stop.

"I meant to do that," he said quickly, trying to look past Ted and see what held his interest.

Ted studied the panels covering this section of the wall. Terry looked up and down the corridor. He could see no other panels. A closed, double-sized hatch was not far away.

"What are we looking at, Ted?" Char asked.

Cory leaned close and put a hand on the back of his shipsuit, hoping to share a little calming energy with him. She couldn't feel him through the suit, so she reached to his neck. He stiffened at her touch, but sighed and his breathing slowed. A slight blue glow surrounded Cory's hand as her nanocytes drifted across his skin.

"What are we looking at?" Char repeated.

"This is the junction that carries much of what comes from in there," Ted answered, pointing toward the hatch without looking at it. He focused on the box he carried in his other arm.

"Pull the panel off," Ted said, waving indiscriminately.

Char looked at it for a moment, gripped it at the bottom, lifted, and popped it outward. The panel came off and she tipped it to the side, letting it drop on the deck.

The area behind the panel was a mass of fiber optics and junction boxes, where bunches of cables entered and different bundles exited.

"No control interface," Ted muttered as he stood and moved close.

Char leaned against the wall next to the opening. She couldn't make heads or tails of what was inside the wall. She shook her head at Terry, and he mirrored her movements. Neither had any idea what it was for.

Cory was ill-equipped for the technology of space. She'd had the option to remain on Earth, but chose to join her parents on their journey to the stars, not because she wanted to learn the ways of spacefarers, but because she believed it was time to leave Earth's future in the hands of others. After she watched so many unenhanced grow old and die, she knew it was time to move on.

It was the curse of the long-lived.

She and the others had to learn new skills. Only Ted seemed to fit in without going through a transition period or training. Maybe he'd always been a spaceman trapped on Earth, and finally, he was free.

"Put an explosive here," Ted said, pointing to a very specific location behind the wall and between fiber optic bundles.

Terry reached into the backpack that Cory carried and

pulled one of the pre-programmed detonators and a blast pack.

"Time or remote detonation?"

"Both. Set for two hours, activate the motion trigger, and keep the remote in your hand," Ted replied.

Terry carefully worked the explosive into the small space. Char picked up the panel and put it back in place.

"What are we afraid of?" Terry asked.

"Intellect." Ted looked at Terry for comprehension, but didn't see any. "Come on. It's time."

Ted walked to the hatch, cycled the wheel, and pushed inward. He went through without waiting for the others.

They hurried after him, rushing through the open hatch and dodging left and right to take up firing positions.

Ted stood, with Plato cradled in his arms, looking up at a swirling blue mass contained within a forcefield.

"I've been expecting you," a voice said.

## Alien Destroyer #1

"I'm getting out of this thing, but I want a mech on our side. Just in case," Marcie said as she parked her suit and climbed out. Kelly's helmeted head nodded, and she punched an armored fist into an armored hand.

"At your service, Colonel," Kelly answered, hoisting her railgun.

Marcie repositioned her brand-new Jean Dukes Special. There was little room inside the armor, so the pistol had been wedged into her stomach and under her ribs. She was happy to be free of the suit.

She liked the firepower it represented, but unlike

Kaeden, she felt stronger when she was more in touch with her surroundings. She closed her eyes and using her heightened senses, pulled power from the Etheric. Marcie searched outward, beyond the airlock, beyond the corridor, and into the ship.

A great ship with a minimal crew. And something else. Something that dabbled in the Etheric, waving to her. Beckoning.

Her eyes shot open, and she stood, mouth agape.

"What is it?" Fitzroy asked, backing away from the hatch leading to the interior of the ship.

"I don't know, but something's waiting for us," Marcie managed to say. She composed herself, dialed her JDS up to six, and stepped boldly into the corridor.

She knew it was empty, and she knew which way to go. She turned left and headed aft.

Kelly signaled for the others to follow, while she stayed close to Marcie. She wasn't sure what her team lead had seen, but the shock on her face was evident. Kelly pointed to her eyes, motioning both ahead and behind.

*Keep your eyes peeled. Stay frosty.*

Marcie strode ahead, shoulders back and head held high. The mech clumped down the corridor, bent slightly to avoid jamming against the ceiling. Fitzroy and Praeter looked over their railgun barrels as they walked, maintaining clear lines of fire past the mech and to the rear.

A hatch opened and a man looked into the corridor. He fell back against the door as Marcie walked up. She shot her fist into the air, giving the signal for the tac team to stop.

"What's your name?" she asked, firmly but softly.

"I'm… I'm…" The man never finished as he stood there, slack-jawed and staring.

"We need to talk with the captain of this boat. Where can we find the captain?" she asked, pointing one way and then the other as she tried to gauge his reaction.

He stood like a stone golem.

"Here's what we're going to do," Marcie started, smiling. "We're going to tie you up and stuff you back in there, and then we're going to continue on our merry way, because you are jack shit for helping us."

Fitzroy squeezed past the mech and turned the man about with an arm bar, then zip-tied him and dumped him unceremoniously back into his workspace, a small electronics repair shop. Fitz secured the hatch on the way out, nodding once to Marcie.

She turned and continued down the corridor, the others stalking after her.

# CHAPTER FIFTEEN

## Alien Destroyer #2

Kaeden looked about, trying to see the cameras or speakers. He didn't expect he'd find a person behind the voice, not in an enclosed space with a well-armed mech.

He wasn't in a hurry to answer, but he'd learned from his parents that talking with the enemy was the best way to defuse a situation or buy time in order to gain an advantage.

"Who do I have the pleasure of addressing?" Kae ventured.

"You can call me Ten," the voice replied.

"Well, Tim," Kae said, purposely mispronouncing the name, "I've got this thing to do, and you're in my way, unless you want to end your blockade, then we can sit down and talk about what started all this and the best way to resolve it while the good people of Alchon Prime get fed."

"Put your weapons down, as a sign of good faith," Ten replied.

Ramses and Gomez had already departed. Capples blocked the hatch, using his armor in case someone tried to lock Kaeden in.

"We're not going to do that." Kae checked his sensors, increasing their sensitivity to look for heat sources, explore the invisible wavelengths, to see what he knew he was missing. He had no course of action besides blowing the ship. He started to wonder if maybe there was another way.

"Am I talking with the ship's captain?" Kae asked.

"We don't have such a thing here. I am controlling the movements of this vessel, if that's what you mean. We know you have people on five of our other ships, by the way. They will all be dealt with in due time."

Kaeden's breath caught, and his heart started to pound. He checked his external comm system, but it was filled with white noise.

*Jamming.*

He tried his comm chip, but none of the other teams replied. They were too far away.

*We're here. We made it about fifty meters and a bulkhead slammed down in front of us. Looks like we're trapped,* Ramses reported.

*Blow it. As much explosives as it takes,* Kae ordered. *Be ready to jump overboard. This fucker is pissing me off, and we're going to start breaking shit until something changes.*

## Alien Ship of the Line #2

Ankh had started at a brisk pace, but was slowing down.

"What's wrong up there?" Christina called, wanting to speed up. She felt that time was not on their side.

"Getting tired," Ankh said over his shoulder.

Christina's jaw dropped. "You have got to be kidding me."

"No. I'm not," Ankh replied matter-of-factly. "Can we take a break?"

"We cannot take a break. It took us too long already. Something is not right."

"Don't be in a hurry to your own funeral," Aaron quoted TH.

"I wish I could put my finger on it, but I can't." Christina shivered. She steeled herself and forced her way past the men up front. They watched her walk, mesmerized. She stopped, having sensed their piercing stares. Half-turning, she growled, "I will rip your fucking eyes out if you keep it up."

Christina's eyes flashed yellow and her claws grew as she changed into her Pricolici form. She looked back at the horrified men, her snout bobbing as she laughed. Effortlessly, Christina scooped up Ankh, taking care not to shred his small body with her claws, and she started running forward.

In that form, she didn't care if the men kept up or not. Ankh had a job to do that he wasn't doing while they were prowling the corridors. Her wolf ears picked up the sound of her team encouraging the men to keep up. They resisted.

They would never be able to look at another woman, should they get the opportunity, without the terror of the unknown beast within rising to torment them.

Christina put everything else out of her mind. She was

the tactical team leader, responsible for accomplishing the mission and bringing her people home alive. Running down the corridor of an enemy ship carrying a small alien while weretigers followed pushing a group of captured humans.

An alien ship crewed by humans. Something that drew the Crenellian and his hacking tools. The faster she ran, the more unease she felt. Christina considered changing back into human form, but discarded the idea.

"Up here!" Ankh said, pointing with one arm while hanging on tightly with the other. His face remained impassive. Christina expected that he liked being carried. His race had no concept of physical fitness. Their bodies had atrophied over time to perform the minimum necessary to support their oversized brains.

Big heads didn't make them smart, as Terry Henry had pointed out on Poddern. It definitely didn't make them more ethical.

Humility was the key to self-improvement. Christina was still new to the Bad Company, but felt right at home. Not a different version of herself, but a better one of her existing person.

One with responsibilities.

She slowed as she approached a large hatch. She sensed the Etheric dimension and discovered that beyond the hatch, something pulled a miniscule amount of energy. She knew that it sensed her coming, just as she had felt its presence.

Christina relaxed and let her body reshape itself into human form. Her custom shipsuit flexed to either form, tightening as she became smaller.

Ankh looked at the wheel in the middle of the hatch. "I've never seen these types of actuators before," he said, before looking back to discover that he was no longer carried by a Were.

"These are common on old Earth ships."

"They aren't like this on the *War Axe*."

"Naval ships. They operate on a planet. In the water," Christina replied.

Ankh looked at her blankly.

"Old Earth mechanical technology to create an airtight or watertight seal. That's all. For such a high-tech alien ship, this is low-tech stuff," Christina stated.

"Maybe it's not a high-tech ship, but a low-tech ship with a high-tech rider," Ankh offered.

Christina looked at the Crenellian and then to the hatch. Aaron and Yanmei ran up. The captives were nowhere to be seen. Christina didn't care that the humans had left. She realized they were irrelevant to accomplishing her mission.

"They bolted at that last intersection," Aaron explained in a low voice, sounding contrite.

"That's fine. They are no threat to us."

"Not anymore," Yanmei replied. Christina's transformation shocked them to their core. They were harmless from that point forward.

"Shall we?" Christina tipped her head toward the hatch. Ankh looked at the wheel in the middle, making no move to turn it. "Fine."

Christina grabbed it and spun it counter-clockwise. She pushed and walked in, one hand on her oversized railgun.

Because one never knew when something needs to be blasted.

## Alien Battleship #1

Joseph staggered, leaning more and more heavily on Petricia. "Hold on, my love," she whispered as she rubbed her cheek on his head.

The vampire in Joseph wouldn't let him quit. The telepath in Joseph was getting overwhelmed. He tried to pull back, but it wouldn't let him go.

His head rocked back from the force of the blow. Petricia yelled. And then his head jerked the other way from a second roundhouse slap.

Auburn winced at the sound his hand made on Joseph's face. Joseph sucked in a great drag of air, as a drowning man who broke the water's surface. His eyes were wide, then cleared as he came back to himself.

Auburn stayed his hand. Petricia stayed hers. Auburn's wake-up call shocked her to the point of her instincts taking over. She was ready to defend her husband, but she'd been too slow. Her vampiric speed had not been there. She waved her hand back and forth, but it didn't accelerate as it should have.

"What is happening to us?" she wondered aloud.

"The Etheric," Kim guessed, watching Petricia test herself.

Bundin ambled up beside them. "Do we not have a ship to subdue?" the Podder asked.

Joseph blinked at the pain remaining in his head. He rubbed one hand across his brow, looking at the sleeve of his shipsuit where he, for a moment, expected to see the black leather that he'd worn for hundreds of years.

"Yes," Joseph started. "We have a mission, and despite the humans, there is an alien. This alien is who we need to confront. I cannot reach out any longer. I'm sorry. Next time, I may not be able to come back."

"No need, Joseph," Kimber told him.

"We will take it from here, my friend," Bundin said, once again using the device attached to the bottom of his shell to speak out loud. He was embracing the vocalization of his thoughts in the human tongue.

Bundin liked the spaceships. It reminded him of Poddern's tunnels, in an odd way, but everything was too bright. He squinted constantly. "When we get back home, I would like sunglasses. My eyes aren't adjusting to the brightness as I expected they would," he accidentally muttered out loud.

Kim wrinkled her forehead. Joseph chuckled while still holding his head.

"Home? You mean to the *War Axe*?" Joseph asked.

"Sorry. I was thinking out loud, I guess, but yes. The *War Axe*. It is comfortable, and I like it there." Bundin was straightforward. He didn't have the capacity for half-truths or mistruths. When he spoke, it was what he believed.

"You're confident we'll be going home, as you call it?" Joseph picked one of the four eyes on Bundin's stalk and looked at it.

"Of course. You freed my people on Poddern, although you were few and your enemies many. You care that people live. I am people. You care that I live, so I trust that you will *make sure* that I live, which means that you will live, because I will not leave your side."

"Holy crap, Bundin! You're going to make me cry," Kim said, looking quickly away.

"That is not my intent, Kimber."

Petricia held onto Joseph's arm with both hands. Auburn looked back and forth, trying to occupy himself with something other than soul-searching.

"You, my friend, have a great attitude. We shall complete our mission and leave this ship alive because it simply cannot be any other way. We will not allow it. *I will not have it!*" Joseph declared, smiling at his friend, before tenderly kissing his wife. "Time to go see what cretin had the audacity to get inside my head."

Joseph and Petricia strolled forward briskly as if walking down a beach on a cool day. Bundin ambled after them. Kimber thumbed her Jean Dukes Special to ten. Looked at it, then dialed it to the max, because, *It goes to eleven.*

Auburn saw what she did and nodded in grim approval. They would take the battleship with them, even if it meant they would not survive. Neither he nor Kim had Bundin's confidence that they would be going home, although the thought of the blue, stalk-headed alien wearing sunglasses was something they both wanted to see.

## Alien Ship of the Line #1

"We've been looking for you, too," Terry said, taking a step forward to stand in front of the group. Some may have considered it arrogance that he stood in front. In his mind, he would be the first to take a bullet if the enemy fired. He would shield those in his charge, but he expected that this entity didn't use bullets. Terry looked around and then stepped back. "I'm Colonel Terry Henry Walton and we've come to end your blockade of Alchon Prime."

"Not wasting any time with the trivialities of your small lives, Colonel Terry Henry Walton," the entity replied.

"Two people become four, then eight, then a nation, and finally a tide that sweeps over a planet and to the stars." Terry rested his hand on his JDS as he studied the containment area. He thumbed the selector to the maximum. He had no doubt the intelligence behind the voice needed to be stopped. His hopes that he could negotiate a settlement had been vastly reduced after the first short exchange. "I see that humans run your ships. Not trivial or indispensable, methinks."

"Run our ships?" the voice questioned. "That is a pedestrian view of what is going on here, but it is the most you are capable of."

"Some are born great, some achieve greatness, and some have greatness thrust upon them," Char offered, quoting William Shakespeare, before adding, "We know what we are, but know not what we may be."

Terry bowed his head in appreciation.

"This is going to be a long day if you are going to insult us instead of getting down to what the hell it is you want. For the life of me, I don't understand why a bunch of pudknockers in souped-up junkers are getting in the way of progress." Terry watched for a reaction, but couldn't tell whether the swirling blue mass changed.

Out of the corner of his eye, Terry could see Ted staring

at the show behind the forcefield. TH expected that Ted was communing with Plato, judging by his blank expression.

"Who is being insulting now?" the voice replied. Terry looked at Char and shrugged. She curled her lip as if to say, *it was worth a try.*

"In our intelligence briefing, someone called you Fuckbert McAssholeface. I have to say that is most unbecoming, so what should we call you?"

"You can call me Ten."

"Ten of twelve? You're not the Borg, are you?"

"Just Ten," the voice replied.

"Well, Ten, we need you to back off and let the cargo ships through. The humans on Alchon Prime need those supplies. Desperately, I might add, because this has gone on for far too long. I appreciate that you didn't openly harm anyone, so maybe that mercy will get you to consider letting a couple ships through, as a sign of good faith."

"As a sign of good faith," Ten repeated. Terry glowered at the nitpicking of his words. "The same good faith that blew up two of our brothers? The same good faith that put your people on five of our other ships? Is that what you are talking about?"

"First rule of negotiation is that no matter how much you hate the fucker on the other side of the table, you have to set that aside in order to move forward. You attacked us, and we blew your shit away. Let it go, and tell me why you're here."

"Because this is where I am," Ten replied in a booming voice.

Char scowled.

Ted continued his stare-down. Cory stood behind the group, fidgeting uncomfortably. The entity was making her hairs stand on end.

"How would your knowing of our purpose be of any help?"

"Our purpose is to restore trade with Alchon Prime. We are going to make sure that happens. There are a couple different ways this can go." Terry left the threat unspoken. He wasn't bluffing, because a JDS dialed to eleven was merciless in its effect. And he'd seen what the *War Axe*'s mains could do to the blockading ships. They could finish the ship from within or without. In either case, the ship was finished.

"Trade will not be restored with the planet you call Alchon Prime. Our reference is Dirikon Four One Seven Zero. The planet is within our space. We have come to secure it from the alien invasion," Ten told them.

"You are staking an ancestral claim to the planet? That's something completely different. Can you show us a celestial map of your territory? No one wants to steal from others."

A holographic projection appeared above their heads. It showed multiple galaxies with billions of planets. Earth, Yol, all explored space was within the projection.

"You have this beater tin can and expect us to believe you control space thousands of light years across? No. My disdain for you is growing by the minute."

*Ted, are you getting anything?* Terry asked using his comm chip.

Ted didn't answer. Char stepped forward.

"I know it is not our place to question your needs or

your authority, but understand that people and other aliens have expanded within this space for thousands of years. I expect you've heard of the Kurtherians. They owned this space for a long time before that."

"The Kurtherians," Ten continued his annoying habit of repeating their words. "What do you know of the Kurtherians?"

"I know that there are fewer of them now than there were a century and a half ago," Terry said, tipping his head back. He wondered if Ten was a Kurtherian, but that couldn't be. Bethany Anne was hunting them. She would not let a Kurtherian so brazenly take up space in her universe.

"A bunch of smart scientist, megalomaniacal types. That's my impression of them. I'm sure you have a different experience, but none of that matters to what is going on this very minute, which is your ships are between the food and the planet. We need to change that status quo."

"We need to change nothing, except to expel your people from our ships. I see the Kurtherian technology coursing through your bodies. You carry the taint of the evil ones."

Terry opened his mouth, but revised what he was going to say. "The enemy of my enemy is my friend. We believe the Kurtherians were evil, too—well, at least some of them. What makes you less evil? In my eyes, you intend to commit genocide of an entire planet. That's pretty fucking evil, if you ask me."

"We are not asking you, Colonel Terry Henry Walton.

We will expedite our recovery of Dirikon Four One Seven Zero."

"Isn't there supposed to be an evil laugh, a mwahaha, or something to that effect?" Terry yawned.

*Ten is an AI,* Terry told Ted.

*Of course Ten is an AI,* Ted replied. *Stop bothering me.*

Terry gave Ted the stink-eye, before returning his attention to the swirling blue mass. His hand never left the butt of his JDS and his eyes remained on the few human crew who stood between him and his target.

# CHAPTER SIXTEEN

**Alien Destroyer #1**

Marcie hugged the exterior corridor and headed aft to the place where she'd seen the ship's engines. If the men escaped, they'd report that she was looking for the captain. She assumed that the captain didn't hang out in the engine room.

Her target was to take out the engines and the ship's power source. Her mission was diversion and distraction. A dead ship would give them pause. A spectacularly exploding ship would draw their attention.

Kelly stayed in the middle, pounding the deck as quietly as she could. She didn't need to turn around to see behind her. She kept the rear screen active in a lower section of her HUD while she focused on navigating the low corridor without stepping on the others.

Fitzroy and Praeter loped behind, their eyes darting up, down, left, and right in a continuous search pattern. They held their railguns up, moving the barrels with their eyes.

Marcie's stride drove her relentlessly toward her goal,

to the heart of the ship, its power, while avoiding the intelligence she'd seen earlier.

She wanted nothing more to do with what she had touched. Marcie was sensitive within the Etheric, a gift that had been passed to her, nurtured, and then her eyes were opened. She had touched evil, and her singular goal had become to kill it.

It was nice that the mission goal overlapped, but Marcie enjoyed Terry's full confidence. If she needed to change the mission, she had the authority to do that.

On her new search and destroy mission, she realized that they wouldn't be going back to the airlock. They'd find a different egress. She stopped, and Kelly almost ran into her.

"Fitzroy and Praeter. Go back and get the mech suit. Fire it up and bring it along. We'll scout up ahead, but won't go too far. At the double-time, gentlemen."

"Yes, ma'am," they replied in unison. They turned and bolted. It wasn't far to the airlock. This was a destroyer, not more than a few hundred feet long.

"Do you want to split us up?" Kelly asked as she watched the two men disappear around a corner. She looked up from the image in her HUD.

"I don't want to, but don't want to lose the progress we've made to get to this point."

Kelly didn't reply to her distracted team lead. It had taken zero effort to get this far. There had been no resistance. Nothing. "Can we at least go back to where we can see them?" Kelly suggested.

Marcie's faced contorted as she struggled with what should have been an easy decision. Kelly reached out her armored hand and grabbed the colonel by the shoulder. "Come on, ma'am. We're going back."

Marcie growled and struggled for a moment, before shaking her head.

"Let's get on our horse. There's some weird shit going on."

To be safe, Kelly blocked Marcie's way aft. The colonel was herself once again and started to run in the direction of the others. They turned two corners, just in time to see a bulkhead drop, cutting them off from the airlock and the other two members of the team.

Marcie lifted her JDS and took aim, but stopped. *Looks like we're cut off,* she said.

*We're at the airlock and Praeter is getting into the suit now,* the sergeant reported.

*New plan. Go outside and head aft, find another way in, which will be our way out. I'm going to blow the engines, so we'll be looking for a quick way off the powder keg. I'm counting on secondaries to send this tub straight to hell.*

Secondary explosions. If the explosives didn't do the trick, she had her JDS.

And it was *dialed to eleven.*

Together, they turned and headed aft. Two corners later, they watched a bulkhead descend and block their way.

Kelly froze in place. Her initial reaction was the feeling of being trapped, until Marcie turned and winked at her. Kelly knew that the colonel couldn't see her face through the helmet.

Marcie casually dialed her JDS to five, aimed at the

middle of the bulkhead, and fired. The metal buckled and twisted, but didn't blow through.

"Disappointing," Marcie said. She thumbed it to seven, braced herself, and fired again. The bulkhead screamed as it was ripped from the superstructure and its shattered remains launched down the corridor.

With her shoulders back and her head held high, she walked through the damaged section, appreciating the power of her new pistol. She picked her way through the wreckage, feeling the alien intelligence's attempts to reenter her mind. But she was blocking, as Joseph had taught her, and she was confident that her actions were her own.

She was confident in her ability to rip the ship apart, piece by piece until with one final blast, it would be relegated to the scrap heap of history.

Marcie's thoughts raced.

*We are outside and heading aft. There's a rupture and the ship appears to be venting atmosphere*, Praeter said.

*Yes, that was us. They tried to block us with another bulkhead. I doubt they'll do that again. Let us know when you've found another way in*, Marcie replied.

"That blast cracked the ship," Marcie said aloud.

Kelly chuckled, the suit's speakers carrying the sound. "Shall we?" she asked, motioning the way ahead using her oversized railgun.

Marcie touched a finger to her forehead in a mock salute before turning and continuing on her mission to destroy the destroyer.

. . .

### Alien Ship of the Line #2

Christina walked through the hatch and stopped as she found a swirling blue mass contained within a forcefield. Ankh leaned around her leg like a small child would.

Aaron and Yanmei held hands as they watched. Ankh pulled an electronics kit from his small backpack and looked for an interface. There were two men in the room, standing at workstations. They stopped what they were doing and looked at the newcomers.

"He's going to need to use your computer," Aaron said pleasantly, approaching the two men. They moved to stand between Aaron and their workstations. Yanmei joined her husband.

"I think he said that we need to use your workstation," she reiterated, smiling at the men.

They turned angry. "What are you doing on this ship?" one demanded.

"Same thing as you, I expect, *living*," she replied.

"We are serving the fleet by working aboard this ship. Women don't belong here. And neither do you other freaks." The man spat his words as if they left a bad taste. He thrust his chest out.

"I think that is enough," a voice said, filling the room with its sound.

"I wondered when you would make an appearance," Ankh said softly before turning to Aaron. "I need access to that terminal, please."

Aaron nodded. He and Yanmei walked forward. The men came at them, but clumsily. The weretigers were martial arts masters from their decades of training in

China. With quick moves, both men were subdued and held with arm bars. Aaron nodded to Ankh.

The Crenellian walked past and touched the screen. The system instantly went dead.

"I'm afraid that I can't let you do that," the voice added.

Christina looked at the swirling mass, knowing intuitively that this was the source of the intelligence.

"My name is Christina and I'm with the Bad Company. We're here to end the blockade of Alchon Prime. How can we proceed in a way that is mutually beneficial?"

"You have destroyed two of our ships and you've put people on five others. I think we are past the mutually beneficial stage, don't you think?" the voice replied.

"I do not think that. When attacked, we defend ourselves. We put people on your ships because there was no other way to talk with you. It is only logical to establish a means of communication in order to negotiate. Other avenues were denied us. We chose the only one in our power to choose."

"I will accept your answer. What do you have that would benefit us?"

"Let's start with your name. I have to be able to call you something as we discuss things."

"You can call me Ten."

"Ten, as in the number?"

"Yes. I thought I enunciated clearly enough."

Christina pursed her lips. Out of the corner of her eye, she saw Ankh under the terminal and digging into the wiring, while Yanmei and Aaron effortlessly restrained the two human members of Ten's crew.

"My apologies." Christina decided on discretion

because it didn't cost her anything. As long as she kept Ten talking, she gave Ankh time to do whatever it was that he did. "Mutually beneficial. I believe access to this sector of space without us blowing your ships out of space is a good start, as long as you pull back the blockade and allow the cargo ships through."

"Giving us what we already have is neither mutual nor beneficial."

"I'm sorry. You already learned that we can kill your ships. So, safe passage isn't something that you already have, and it's only the first thing that comes to mind, but we need to talk and find out what is beneficial. So how about this—instead of me guessing what you want, I'll tell you what we would like, and then you tell us what you would like. We'll see what might be palatable, and then we can take it upstairs. I'll start. We need to feed the people on Alchon Prime. The cargo ships are sitting at the edge of the heliosphere. We would like you to let them through."

"You speak in odd expressions. Palatable and upstairs. We have neither," Ten replied. Christina waited. "You have to leave our space. That is our one and only term."

"You see? That wasn't too hard. I would have never come up with that on my own because it's way out there. Your space is the area around Alchon Prime? I'm not sure if we're good with resettling a whole planet. I'd have to check on that, but look! We're making progress. Thank you, Ten," Christina said with an exaggerated nod.

"Our space is this and the adjoining galaxy. You must leave these two galaxies immediately." A starfield appeared above the group as a holographic image.

Christina studied it before looking to Aaron and

Yanmei. Ankh was occupied beneath the station. He had wires tapped into a portable computer.

"That appears to be the entirety of the pan and loop galaxies, which I believe represents billions of systems, including Earth. I'd like to discuss the logistics of completing your request further, but that would probably take a hundred million years to accomplish. I don't have that much time, either to discuss or execute."

Christina thought that Ten deserved a profanity-laden tirade. Once again, she chose a different tack.

"You are pretty, if you don't mind me saying. The way the blue ebbs and flows within your shell, well, it's pretty."

## Alien Ship of the Line #1

"Bullshit dribbles from your digital puss like water over a fall. What an ass-monkey, and for the record, you are one ugly motherfucker!" Terry shouted. *Ted, I'm running out of stupid shit to say. Are you about done?*

Terry flipped the double bird to the swirling blue that he equated with the entity called Ten. Char rolled her eyes and shook her head.

Cory held her hands up in surrender. "Dad, are you okay? If you're having a brain aneurysm or something, I can help."

Terry's tongue was hanging out of his mouth as he flopped his head onto his shoulder. He made eye contact with Cory long enough to wink at her.

She wasn't buying it. He looked too natural in the role he was playing.

The lights in the space flashed red, and they thought

they heard a scream that came from within their souls. Terry stopped his antics and looked at Char and Cory. They both shook their heads.

Ted smiled. The other three watched him carefully. *Ted?*

*We're in,* Ted replied. He tipped his chin toward the corner. *And for the record, Ten is over there, behind that casing. You're giving the finger to the ship's engine.*

Terry wondered how long Ted had known, but thought it best not to ask. He was perpetually mad at Ted, but it helped that no matter where they went, Ted was always the smartest guy in the room. He understood the werewolf. Despite his foibles, Ted worked in the best interests of humanity.

And his friend Plato seemed to be aggravating Ten.

*The enemy of my enemy,* Terry thought, smiling as the AIs fought somewhere in a nebulous digital world.

At least that was how he envisioned it.

"You will stop your inane attempts to reach me," Ten demanded.

"You didn't want to discuss the situation," Terry said seriously. "You only wanted to play word games. We were never here to play. We will end this blockade, and we will end it today."

"You have no ability to end the blockade."

"Your underpowered, old technology ships are going to stop us? Who do you think you're talking to? You may be somewhere in your own version of a higher evolutionary scale, but your ships? They are going to blow up quite nicely."

*They are launching their fighter drones. Kill the engine,* Ted insisted.

"Hoods!" Terry shouted as he took aim. At the last second, he remembered to dial it back. Char turned and dove at Cory. Terry set his JDS to eight and pulled the trigger.

The room filled with the inferno of the exploding engine.

# CHAPTER SEVENTEEN

**Alien Destroyer #1**

Another bulkhead dropped and Marcie laid waste to it. The setting on the JDS was appropriate for ripping metal from the inside of the spaceship without tearing too-big holes in the superstructure.

When the corridor dead-ended, Marcie started opening hatches. She found men cowering within. She ignored them, shutting the hatch and spinning the wheel to close them before the men started ogling.

Kelly mirrored Marcie's actions until the mech warrior found what they were looking for. "In here, ma'am. I think this is it."

Marcie strode boldly down the corridor. Kelly leaned back, one armored arm outstretched to hold the hatch open. Inside were banks of sealed systems above which a small blue shape swirled. Marcie pulled her hood into place.

"Stand back," she said.

"You don't want to do that," a voice said, booming within the space. Marcie dialed to eight.

"Sure I do." She took aim.

"NOOOO!" the voice screamed.

Marcie fired. Kelly tried to close the hatch before the fireball reached them, but flames launched through the opening at the speed of light, blowing Marcie against the bulkhead. Tendrils of smoke drifted from her shipsuit. Her bubble-helmet was contorted, half-melted from the heat.

Kelly made sure the hatch was closed as she grabbed Marcie under her armpits and stood her up. "Look at me."

"I am. It's this melted hood. You think your railgun will blow a hole in the side of this thing so we can get out of here?" Marcie asked.

The lights flickered and went out. The passageway was lit by a soft red glow.

"Wait," Marcie said.

Marcie sniffed, wrinkling her face as she smelled something that shouldn't have been there. "Damn. Suit's compromised," she said, pinching at a tear along her abdomen. Then a second appeared and a third.

"Why didn't you use explosives?" Kelly asked.

"Next time, we'll do just that, but the mission was to create a diversion, and then I touched its mind, Kelly. That thing was the darkest evil I've ever seen, and I've been face to face with Forsaken."


**The *War Axe***

"Enemy fighters launching!" K'Thrall announced as he

brought up his holographic defense grid. He started cycling through his weapon systems to double-check availability.

"All hands to battle stations. Prepare for incoming fighter spacecraft," Micky said over the ship-wide broadcast. He knew that people were starting to run through the corridors on their way to their work or damage control locations.

The bridge crew pulled their hoods into place. Micky watched the main screen, almost forgetting to join the others. He pulled the clear hood over his head. It snapped into place, then filled with air as the suit pressurized. Gloves slid from the sleeves and settled in around his fingers.

When the gloves were in place, they felt like a second skin. He never minded being contained within the atmosphere of his shipsuit. It was a way of life for the spacefaring. It also put his mind at ease that he wouldn't die instantly if there was a hull breach. He'd linger.

"K'Thrall. Report to the combat operations center. Join Commander Mac and prepare to fight the ship," Micky directed.

The Yollin finished running his preparations, then headed off the bridge, all four legs pumping as he ran. Three decks down, buried in the heart of the ship, was where the fights happened. Micky had grown comfortable on the bridge, which was survivable in its own right, but not like the COC. When all else failed and the ship was shattered into a million pieces of space debris, the COC would keep those within alive.

*And that's why I can't go in there. A captain should go down with his ship,* Micky thought. *If I kill the* War Axe, *then I should die with her.*

"Well, Clifton, what do you say we move into more open space. Give us a little room to maneuver."

"Yes, sir," the helm officer replied. He tapped his screens to activate the engines. Thrusters maintained the ship's attitude as the *War Axe* smoothly accelerated.

"Thirty degrees up on the bow," Micky ordered. "Let's get out of the system's rotational plane."

"Ship is answering thirty degrees," helm replied. Micky sat back and watched the screens showing the immensity of space. The combat projection showed a small swarm of fighters heading their way.

"Smedley, are those all of the enemy fighters?"

"One ship's worth. The second ship of that configuration did not launch any spacecraft. Standby... I see massive explosions on one of the alien destroyers, the one to which Colonel Marcie Walton's team deployed." Smedley kept his voice neutral to avoid exciting the bridge crew with the potentially bad news.

"I think our people have delivered their calling card," Micky said slowly, looking at the enhanced images shared on the main screen. The explosion tore a hole in the aft end of the ship. After a few minutes, secondary explosions ripped the tin can apart. "Tell me that our people got off."

"I cannot. We have no way of knowing, not at this distance."

"Holy shit," Micky muttered. He closed his eyes and said a short prayer for the Company and the crew. "The new battle has begun. Let us end it. Right here, right now."

. . .

## Alien Battleship #2

Timmons's team roamed the corridors like a bully gang from high school.

One of the crew appeared and held out a hand to stop the four, but dropped it when he looked at Sue.

"You have an admirer, my dear," Timmons said through clenched teeth. His blood continued to pound. The werewolf grabbed the man and shoved him against the wall. "Where's the captain? Where's the person in charge?"

The man stuttered and stammered. "A woman…"

"What? You act like you've never seen a woman before."

"I haven't. No one has."

The color drained from Timmons's face. "How could you not see a woman? Are you a clone?"

"I am the ship's crew," the man replied as if that told the whole story.

"What's that have to do with anything?" Sue asked.

The man's mouth hung open as he looked at her.

"You can stop that shit right now," she snarled. Nothing changed.

"What do you mean you've never seen a woman? Explain," Timmons demanded.

"Those not selected for breeding are given other tasks deemed critical for the home world. Serving on a spaceship is one of them. Those selected train their entire lives for duties in space."

"So, the ones who work—get all studly, are the good providers—are denied women. That is a really fucked-up society," Merrit mumbled. Shonna elbowed him, but her lip curled as she glared at the crewman.

"We aren't worthy," the man replied, as if quoting scripture.

"Did you know we were on board?" Timmons asked, trying to change the subject.

"No." The man looked uncomfortable. Timmons was using his body to block the man's view of the Were females.

"Good. You are going to take us to the captain so we can have ourselves a conversation, first about that little high-speed pass stunt, and then about the continued existence of this ship."

"I cannot."

"Refusing to cooperate?" Timmons loomed over the man, leaning close as he tried to intimidate the weaker human.

"No," he said, barely above a whisper. "I don't know what that is."

"How about the person in charge?" Timmons studied the man's features, trying to determine if the crewman was lying.

"There is no person in charge. We perform designated tasks." The man pulled an electronic pad from a cargo pocket on his coveralls. He showed the screen to Timmons.

It took his chip a second to translate what he saw. "This is a maintenance work order and station assignment." Timmons took the pad from the man. He reached out to take it back, but Sue slapped his hand away.

Timmons tapped the screen. "Schematics. Step-by-step repair procedures. Most of this stuff is basic. Here's a little more involved work, here, but even Merrit could do this stuff." Timmons smiled at his old friend.

"Who issues the tasks?" Sue asked, pointing to the pad.

"They come through, on there, whenever we complete a task." The crewman nodded toward the screen as he started making cow eyes at Sue. She gagged and stepped back.

"Are you thinking what I'm thinking?" Shonna asked, as one engineer to another. Merrit was a chemist and Sue had specialized in public administration, but Shonna and Timmons both had degrees and extensive experience as engineers.

"I expect that I am," Timmons said over his shoulder. "Where's the computer that runs this ship? We would like to talk with it."

The ships lights flashed and it lurched briefly before the artificial gravity compensated. "What's going on?" Sue demanded, lunging for the man.

"We're taking action to protect the fleet," the man replied, his head tilted slightly as he gazed adoringly at Sue.

"Take us to the computer. NOW!"

"We're behind schedule," Merrit interjected. "The fight is getting underway."

"And we're still fucking around like rats in a maze," Timmons growled. He grabbed the man and propelled him in the direction the two men had been heading. "RUN, motherfucker!"


## Alien Destroyer #2

Capples remained in the open hatch, his armor a buttress against Kaeden getting trapped within the space.

Kae held the explosives in his hand as he looked for a

place to put them. A computer terminal stood to his left and to his right, where there were contained systems. More important than what he could see was what he couldn't see. *A power distribution grid.*

It had to be outside the engine or generator and more vulnerable. That was Kae's reasoning.

His suit's sensors couldn't find anything. Kae dropped a bundle of explosives on each side of a large structure he guessed was the engine, and then he raised his railgun.

"Say good-bye."

The lights went out and a soft red glow bathed the space. Kaeden smirked. The suit compensated and on his HUD, it appeared as if nothing had changed. A hum grew from within the engine.

"We are taking action against those who have infiltrated our ships," the voice said calmly.

An explosion rocked the destroyer.

*The bulkhead is no more,* Gomez reported.

"You're doing a crap job of that, it appears," Kaeden snarked. "You have no internal security."

"There was no need. The crew follows orders. We had not anticipated single-entity penetration of our perimeter. We shall not make that mistake again," the voice replied like it was clinically discussing the engagement as part of an after-action review. Kae wondered if there was coffee and doughnuts.

Suddenly, he felt hungry and wondered when the last time he'd eaten was.

"I expect you won't get the opportunity to share your experience. Cap, we're leaving." Kaeden backed up until he blocked the hatch. Capples turned and headed down the corridor.

"Tell your mom I said hi," Kae added as he fired at the systems, using the rapid-fire setting of his oversized railgun to rip the components to shreds. Sparks and metal shards flew. Kae adjusted and lit up the computer terminal and random equipment around it with a few dozen small projectiles accelerated to hypervelocity.

Kae slammed the hatch and cycled the action. Using his eyes, he brought up the remote activator for the explosives, set it for two minutes, and virtually mashed the button.

He ducked as he jogged up the corridor. *Get on your horse, Cap. Big boom's coming.*

## Alien Battleship #1

Joseph stood before the hatch leading to an interior section. Petricia knew his look. She nodded.

"Maybe it's okay not to live forever," she told him. "It's important who you die with, but what matters most is who you live with. Thank you for helping me to feel alive again."

Joseph blinked quickly to fight off the tears. He had come from a patriarchal society where it wouldn't do to cry in front of the ladies. Petricia was fine with it, as she knew the depth of his personality. That he cared.

Bundin caught up with them. "Shall we?" the Podder asked, wondering about the delay.

"Of course," Joseph conceded. He made eye contact with Kim and Auburn. They both nodded their approval.

Joseph took a deep breath and turned back to the hatch. He opened it and walked through, Petricia close behind. Bundin followed, while Kim and Auburn watched from the opening.

"We're here, but you already knew that," Joseph announced.

The group had grown adept at ignoring the distraction as the klaxons continued to sound and the lights flashed.

"Welcome, Joseph. Our time together was refreshing," a disembodied voice announced. A forcefield held a swirling blue mass tightly. Machines stood at either end of the field, but they made no sound. The hairs on Joseph's head stood on end.

"There is power in this room," Joseph said, stating the obvious. Physical power and computing power that supported the intelligence that had invaded Joseph's mind. He wondered aloud, "What secrets remain?"

"I think none," the voice replied.

"That is where you are wrong," Bundin said, wedging his way beside Petricia. "What you don't know is what these good people are capable of doing in defense of those who can't protect themselves. The secret that remains is how long you are going to try and drag this out, because you will fall, inevitably, to the humans."

"We use humans. That is why we acquired them, and that is all they are good for. Poddern, also called Tissikinnon Four. Our designation is Dirikon Zero Three Zero One. We will eradicate all life on that planet. Your species serves no useful purpose."

Bundin's stalk remained steady. He unblinkingly looked at the blue mass. "As I said, it is only how long you linger before you expire."

"What will it take to break the blockade?" Kim called from the corridor.

"You will remove the infestation on Dirikon Four One Seven Zero. You must evacuate the planet you call Alchon Prime. This is our space, and that is our one condition. You know what it's like to go to someone else's land, encroaching until the natives have been pushed out, don't you, Joseph?"

"America. The natives were unarmed for the battle waged against them," Joseph intoned. He let go of Petricia's hand, running his fingers up her arm until he could squeeze her shoulder. He stepped forward and started to pace. "But that isn't here, and you aren't native to this system. I venture that you aren't native to this galaxy. Bundin is here, an emissary of his free people. This is far different."

"You argue with yourself, Joseph. I saw your mind and all that you are. A vampire. A poet. A warrior. A peacemaker. No. You will take your ship and go, or we will eliminate every living creature in this system, and you will be gone all the same."

"I'm not sure how you're going to do that," Kim said, shaking her head. "You can't even keep a few meat-sacks off your ship, so I think you are all bluster. Time for you to leave and not come back."

Auburn checked the corridor, expecting a security force, but none came.

The fight was within.

"What weapon does it have that we don't know about?" he whispered into Kim's ear.

She shook her head and mouthed, "Is it bluffing?"

CHAPTER EIGHTEEN

## Alien Ship of the Line #1

The air cleared as the fire suppression system kicked in. Terry gasped in pain. Char and Cory were both down. Ted was hunched over the box that carried Plato. Terry tried to holster his JDS, but the holster was misshapen, distorted by the intensity of the heat.

"Char," he grunted, as he crawled across the floor. The air shimmered from the residual heat. Charumati was lying atop their daughter, the back of her suit melted and torn. The delicate skin underneath was similarly torn. Terry cradled her body as he gently rolled her toward him. Her bubble-helmet was gone. Much of her hair was gone.

The smell of burnt hair and flesh permeated the space. Cory blinked as she rolled out from under her mother. She pulled her hood off and with calm concern, jumped to her mother's aid.

"She'll be fine," Cory said, as much to herself as to her father. Terry couldn't leave go. "Check on Ted," Cory managed to say.

Terry hesitated, watching the blue glow of Cory's hands as it danced across Char's scorched head and down the shredded skin of her back.

"You're next, Dad," Cory said softly.

"You take care of your mother. I'll be fine." Terry winced as he fought against the pain. He carefully moved out from under Char and stood, his skin protesting the movement. His chest looked like a pig's after spending too much time on the spit.

He stumbled, gritted his teeth as he looked for an enemy, and continued on. Ten had been silenced, but Terry wasn't convinced that he was gone.

Terry found Ted barely conscious. Although his injuries were less than what Char and Terry had suffered, he was in agony.

"Talk to me, Ted. Let's see those yellow eyes of yours."

Ted struggled and his eyelids fluttered. He couldn't focus when he finally managed to keep his eyes open. "Did you know it was going to blow like that?"

"Yes," Ted mumbled.

"Then why?" Terry pressed.

"You have no idea what Ten is. A consciousness beyond an AI. Something with a black heart that is not driven by logic. It needs to die, but killing this ship won't kill it. Its consciousness is split throughout the fleet," Ted explained, his breathing steadying the more he talked.

"I have no intention of dying, Ted, but if we are going to end this thing, then we'll go where we have to go, do what we have to do. Did the ship launch its fighters?"

"It did not," Ted replied with a half-smile, before turning ominous. "Plato says that Ten is still here."

Terry leaned Ted against an equipment bank. He hurried back to where he'd left his JDS on the deck. He picked it up and looked at Char. She smiled back at him. Cory continued to work on Char's back.

"Ten is still here," he whispered. He caressed the side of her head as he looked into her eyes. The purple was there, but the usual sparkle was gone. He nodded tersely before standing up. He stepped carefully across the room. "You said it was in here?"

Terry pointed his pistol at the equipment bank Ted was leaning against. Ted struggled to pull himself upright.

"Plato is collecting a little more information. When he's done, I'll let you know. We are using a scalpel to deal with this situation, while you," Ted said with renewed brashness, "you are using a steamroller."

Terry smiled. "Yes, I am. Tell Plato to pick up the pace. The longer we let this thing live, the more damage it can cause. On a completely different note, does it separate the men and women simply to torture and control the men?"

Ted looked to Cory and Char. "That would be the most likely reason based on what we have seen within the entity."

"Ten is an asshole just to be an asshole." Terry leaned around the equipment panel, surprised that he didn't see any lights, despite Ted's assurances that Ten was alive. "Fuckbert McAssholeface. Holy shit. It has lived down to the name we gave it."

"Oddly enough, but it has been like it is for thousands of years. And despite what it said, it has no claim over this system. It's only here to see people die horribly. We surprised it, and it is still looking for an answer to us."

"This stupid fucker thought it was going to blockade a planet and no one was going to help?"

"Had we not agreed, then no. No one would have come to help them. The people of Alchon Prime would have died, and Ten would have taken great pleasure in watching."

"Move out of the way and let me kill this thing," Terry snarled.

## Alien Ship of the Line #2

A scream of rage filled the space, threatening to crush all within. Christina, Aaron, and Yanmei covered their ears. The Crenellian was not quick enough. He howled in pain as he fell to the deck and rolled around, holding his head.

The sound tapered off until it was only a whimper.

"Ten? How are you doing, buddy?" Christina asked, tentatively removing her hands. Aaron and Yanmei hurried to help Ankh. The small humanoid sat up and blinked away the remaining pain.

Yanmei gave him a brief hug before he went back to work. The weretigers stood between him and the swirling blue mass.

"What have you done?" Ten asked accusingly.

"We are here in this space trying to learn more about you and where you come from so we can discuss how to end the blockade," Christina replied innocently.

"Meat-bags. Fuckbert. Infiltrators. Infestation. Aliens. Evil. Who is evil? You are trying to kill us, all that is me. You are killing humans, those who serve. They are no threat to you, but you kill them nonetheless." The last syllable hung in the air.

Christina looked around as if weapons would appear from the walls and turn the room into a shooting gallery. She caught Ankh's furious movements as he tapped and interfaced with his computer tablet hardwired into the terminal.

"Where did you hear the word 'Fuckbert'?" Aaron asked.

Ten didn't bother to answer. Christina took the cue. "Let me talk to my friends on the other ships so we can stop anything that might be going on. Then we can talk on even terms."

"It is too late to talk. Soon, your ships will be destroyed. Know that in your failure, you will have killed all the people on Dirikon Four One Seven Zero, the planet you call Alchon Prime." The voice disappeared.

"Ten?" Christina tried. "Ankh, do you have anything for us? Is the alien fleet attacking the *War Axe*?"

Ankh tapped away, oblivious to everything around him. Christina walked over to him, bending down to peer under the terminal. "Ankh?"

"This ship has launched all its fighters, and they are on their way to attack the *War Axe*. The rest of the alien fleet is starting to move."

"Recall the fighters, Ankh!"

The Crenellian tapped away. He stopped and held the device against his head.

"Osmosis?" Christina whispered over her shoulder, glancing around the space. The blue swirled behind the forcefield without interruption.

"New chip," Yanmei replied. "Does he have to hold his tablet like that?"

Christina shook her head. She had grown up with technology, so it was second nature to her, and that put her well ahead of the rest of Terry's people when it came to the learning curve. But Ankh was a new addition, albeit coming from a technologically advanced race.

His chip had recently been upgraded from the standard translation device to a much more powerful cyber-interface, the likes of which Ted built for himself. Ankh had always trusted his oversized brain. It wasn't natural for him to share his thought process. Ted embraced the partnership, never relinquishing control.

Ankh was still learning. His manual interface had been too slow. Christina smiled. *Helping the team on their journey of self-improvement,* she thought.

"Ten? What are you doing, buddy? We can't have a shooting war, I hope you understand. It makes it much harder to talk." Christina put her hands on her hips and frowned. The conversation was over. The others had gone into action and Ten was fighting back.

"Place the explosives," she said, resigned with the final course of action. "Ankh, if you can't get control of those fighters, get what you can and get the hell out of there."

**Alien Destroyer #1**

Kelly parked the mech and opened the back, hurriedly climbing out. "Get in," she said.

"I can't ask you to do this," Marcie said.

"One of us is going to be outside in a shipsuit, regardless. It really should be the one with an intact system. I know you never would have ordered it."

Marcie didn't hesitate. She climbed in, ignoring the sweat that lined the inside of the suit. She buttoned it up, and Kelly pulled her hood into place.

"Climb on," Marcie told her using the suit's external speakers.

Kelly jumped onto the mech's back, ducking below the helmet so she wouldn't get her head taken off as Marcie ran through the corridor.

The eerie red glow continued. Klaxons rang throughout the ship.

*I'd try to blow a hole in the side of this thing, but if we can make the airlock, then we'll take that route. Fitzroy. Praeter. Where are you guys?*

*Inside the airlock, suited up and ready to go. We had to chase some of the crew away. They were a bit panicked.*

*Did you tell them to get to their lifeboats?*

*They didn't seem to know what those were...* Fitzroy let the thought linger.

*YOU CANNOT ESCAPE!* boomed into Marcie's mind. She gasped, staggered, and fell.

*I live in the shell of my mind. I am me and no one else,* Marcie repeated over and over, an exercise that Joseph and Akio had both taught her. The pain in her head lessened, but Ten had a foothold. Marcie was holding the entity at bay, but able to do nothing else.

"Uh, boss, we need to get going," Kelly said, still clinging to the mech's back. An explosion shook the ship. The red lights dimmed until the corridor was bathed in darkness. Kelly closed her eyes, willing her night vision to hurry up.

*I live in the shell of my mind. I live in the shell of my mind...*

## The *War Axe*

"Blanket the incoming with plasma rounds. See if we can channel them into a kill zone," Micky ordered.

Clifton maintained watch of the helm, but weapons control drove the thrusters to adjust the weapons' aim. The ship's nose curled in a tiny circle as the mains fired a twin stream of plasma rounds, bracketing the alien fighters.

"Cease fire," Micky said. The fighters had scattered, doing the opposite of what the skipper intended. "When will they be in range, Smedley?"

"Less than two minutes, Skipper."

Dokken howled beyond the hatch to the bridge.

"Open the hatch and let him in, Smedley," the captain said softly, turning to see Dokken trot in. He dog-smiled at Micky before joining Clifton up front. "You don't usually come to the bridge."

*I have nowhere else to go. Can you make me a suit so I can join my goofy human next time?* Dokken looked at the captain with sad brown eyes.

"I think we can do that, Dokken. You are welcome up here any time. Do you know where Wenceslaus is? I expect he's a bit lonely, too."

*If I knew that, I wouldn't be here. He would be cowering in terror as I brought the full wrath of my species upon his arrogant orange head!* Dokken proclaimed.

"He's in the engine space, isn't he, Smedley?"

"He is," the EI admitted. Micky didn't press it.

"You need to become friends with Lieutenant Clodagh,

Dokken," Micky advised, watching the ship icons peppering the main screen. "We will take the War Axe into battle. Prepare to fight the ship. Bulkheads are in place. Weapons are hot. K'Thrall, you have the trigger. Fire when ready."

A starfield of outgoing rounds from a hundred railguns appeared around the ship. Missiles launched, disappearing after the initial engine burn, before the gravitic drives took over.

The *War Axe* turned sharply away from the incoming fighters and headed directly toward Alchon Prime.

---

Lieutenant Clodagh Shortall stood at her workstation as she monitored the engines. A full barrage from both the mains and the close-in systems drove energy usage toward the ninetieth percentile.

The ship was designed to handle the surges. It wasn't designed for sustained performance at that drain. The main engines accelerated the huge ship forward, jinking and darting at irregular intervals. The main engines welcomed the challenge.

"It looks like we're giving them a big, hairy what-for!" she exclaimed, looking down at the orange cat curled onto a soft bed beneath her station. She adjusted coolant flows based on Smedley's recommendations.

The ship rocked and a dull boom reverberated through the space. One of the thrusters spiked red as it burned out. The board showed red. "Dispatch repair bot to replace damaged thruster," she told her board. With deft taps on her console, she jettisoned the dead thruster into space and input the location and thruster type for the repair bot. The stores database confirmed that replacements were on hand and stored within that bulkhead-sealed section.

All was in order. Clodagh wondered what was on the menu for dinner. She wanted to pull it up, but the ship lurched again, then started to roll.

CHAPTER NINETEEN

## Alien Destroyer #2

Cap ran like a madman, leaping the wreckage that the other two warriors had left with their discriminating use of too much explosives on offending bulkheads.

Kaeden's mech pounded down the corridor. He ran through the wreckage without seeing any of the human crew.

The humans were going to die. Kae slowed. Cap pressed forward until he couldn't hear the major behind him. He stopped and turned, waving at Kaeden to catch up.

"How can we get the humans off?" Kae asked, walking forward.

"We can't," Cap replied tersely. "They work for the enemy. They killed a couple cargo ships and they almost killed the *War Axe*. They are the enemy."

"They're human. I say they were raised wrong." Kae and Capples were thrown from their feet. The ship cried out in its death throes, shaking furiously.

"We need to go," Cap said.

"We need to find out where their home planet is," Kae said, before nodding. "Belay that. We need to get the hell out of here."

He jumped to his feet and started to jog ahead. Cap turned and sprinted, staying barely ahead of the powered armor.

*I hope the data mining teams were successful,* Kae thought. *Collateral damage. Innocent bystanders. Victims. Fuck.*

"It sucks that we can't save them all," Kae growled.

"The missions are designed to save as many as possible," Cap said over his shoulder in between taking great gulps of air. "I wouldn't want to be your dad. He carries the responsibility for every casualty on his shoulders."

"As much as we tell him not to."

"As much as I'm suggesting that you don't either." Cap slowed as he reached the airlock. Ramses was holding the hatch open with an armored glove. The two final members of the tac team climbed through. They cycled the hatch and punched the button to depressurize the space.

The lights flashed on the panel and went out. The air stopped hissing and both hatches remained firmly in place.

## Alien Battleship #2

Timmons ran with one hand on the crewman's back, forcing him to run at a breakneck pace.

The tac team followed, watching for an attack from the ship's internal security force.

"How far?" Timmons demanded.

The man's breathing was ragged, his face splotchy. Sweat poured down his head. They'd been running for a total of one minute. As the man turned to answer, he drifted to the side of the corridor and ran headlong into a half-opened hatch.

The hollow sound of a melon being dropped on a sidewalk made the werewolves wince. Timmons lithely danced past the obstruction, stopping to look back at the crewman, out cold with a bump growing on the side of his head.

"Merrit can take care of the next one," Sue offered. "You seem to have damaged yours."

Timmons smirked and shook his head. "We have to be close. Everyone spread out and find the guts of this bitch."

"Found it," Shonna called after two seconds. She opened an interior hatch, showing a blue light dancing within.

"What's that?" Sue asked.

"I suspect it's the power source for the ship. See the shimmer? There's a forcefield around it. I'd call it a containment field," Shonna explained.

Timmons glanced at the man on the deck, shrugged, and headed for the doorway that Shonna and Merrit were stepping through. "Watch our six," he said to Sue.

She nodded and took a position in the corridor. Timmons joined the other two. Shonna had approached and was studying the forcefield and swirling blue mass within. A bank of human-sized workstations stood to the left. Timmons went there, surveying the screens. He was surprised to find that he could understand the language, but the new chip in his head translated it for him.

He reached a finger toward the screen to start searching for information they would find useful. It went blank before he touched it. Timmons jammed his finger into the place where the icon had been. The other screens were blank, too.

"Someone knows we're here, and it's watching us," Timmons said loudly, hoping his revelation would encourage the enemy to show itself. He already knew that the ship was run by an AI. What he didn't know was who programmed it.

Shonna reached out toward the forcefield, close but taking care not to touch it. "There's a lot of power in this," she said. "I think if it loses containment, the whole ship would be lost."

Timmons joined her for a closer look.

"Is that the plan?" Merrit asked.

"It could be, depending on whether we can talk with this thing or not. We need tricorders or something," Timmons said.

"When we see the *Enterprise,* I'll ask if they have one we can borrow," Shonna replied.

"Or we can ask Ted," Timmons countered. "R2D2 has to have something, don't they? Maybe we can ask Fuckbert, since they seem to have acquired some R2D2 technology?"

Shonna didn't have a comeback for that. She nodded slowly as she moved away from the forcefield and began searching the rest of the space.

"Fuckbert? Are you there? We want to talk with you."

They felt the ship start to move. Shonna pulled a toolkit from her small backpack and started loosening an equipment cover. "Recalcitrant little bastard," she mumbled as she called on her werewolf strength break the bolts free. She pried and snapped them, one after another.

Her face turned red as she grunted with her efforts. Timmons watched.

"Give me a hand," she called after breaking the last fastener. Together, they lifted the cover free, exposing an exotic system within. "I think we found our alien."

Timmons caressed his oversized railgun. It would be so easy to blast it and be done with the alien. He raised the barrel. "I know you can see us. If you don't want to talk, then you leave us no other course of action."

"You will leave this place," a voice said, filling the space with sound.

"My name is Timmons. We need you to end your blockade. We are willing to trade some very fancy beads," he said. Shonna stood and punched him in the arm. "What? We are from New York. I thought that's how we did business."

"You have nothing that we want," the voice replied.

"The alternative is that you have something that we can take away, which, in essence, is something that you want— for us not to destroy your ships that are carrying AIs. Each dead ship means a dead AI. That's what we're willing to trade. The blockade will end either way. Your choice is limited to whether you wish to survive it or not. You have one minute to answer." Timmons crossed his arms as he assumed his waiting-impatiently pose.

Shonna held her hands up and mouthed, "What the fuck?"

Timmons smirked and mouthed back, "I have a plan."

Sue swore that she could hear Shonna's eyes roll. Sue shook her head, standing in the doorway and taking it all in. Merrit had crawled under the terminal and opened a panel.

"Anything good?" Timmons asked while waiting for the alien to answer.

"Nah. Just a bunch of wires and stuff. I was hoping to see memory chips or a hard drive or something that we could snag, give to Ted for him to examine later."

"A hard drive?" Timmons asked. "When's the last time you saw a hard drive?"

"I think that you should die. Your ship will die. All the cargo ships will die, and in the end, we will watch the people of Dirikon Four One Seven Zero slowly starve to death. And it will be your fault."

"You were starving them to death before we got here. Since then, you're down two ships, and we're standing here, looking at your ugly ass. See this?" Timmons waggled his fingers in the direction of the system that Shonna had exposed. "This is me waving good-bye."

Timmons motioned for the others to leave, making a fist and then flashing his fingers in what he thought they'd interpret as an order for them to get their explosives ready. Instead, they ran from the space and disappeared down the corridor. "Get back here and set your explosives!" Timmons bellowed.

He ducked his head, expecting the entity to attack him in some way. "What? No internal security systems?" Timmons blurted.

The alien didn't bother to answer.

"Holy shit! You don't have any because you never considered the possibility." Timmons laughed as he pulled a small pack of explosives from his backpack. He set the timer for five minutes, but didn't activate it. "I expect your IQ is twenty billion, but you haven't figured out humans. Welcome to the party, pal." Timmons placed the explosive beneath the forcefield holding the swirling blue mass in place.

Shonna and Merrit showed up and sheepishly deposited their packages.

"Five minutes," Timmons told them.

Shonna slid one of her bundles next to what they assumed was the AI.

"No need. I got that one covered," Timmons said, patting his railgun. She slapped him on the shoulder and ran from the space a second time. "Sue, if you'll do the honors. Start the countdown."

Sue pulled the activation device from her pocket and held her thumb on it to activate it, touched the start button, and watched the numbers count backward from five-zero-zero.

"Countdown has begun," she reported.

"Fire in the hole!" Timmons yelled before backing into the corridor. The stream of hypervelocity projectiles ripped into the system. The werewolf within sensed the waves of energy released into the Etheric. Timmons stopped firing so he could gather his wits. He shook his head to clear it.

One last look showed that the damage was complete. Timmons shouldered his railgun and jogged after the others. He heard Shonna's railgun barking up ahead.

He tried to blink the fog away, but it remained. He gritted his teeth and forced himself to run faster.

. . .

## Alien Battleship #1

Joseph's eyes rolled back in his head as he fell. Petricia caught him and eased him to the deck.

Bundin moved forward to stand over the unconscious vampire, protecting him with his shell. Kim and Auburn raised their weapons. "What is it, Petricia? What happened?"

"We need to get him out of here." She pulled him by the arms, dragging him toward the corridor. Bundin moved enough to stay between Joseph and the swirling blue mass.

"Blow it?" Kim asked Auburn. He held one hand with the palm upward and shrugged.

"I'll take that as a yes," she replied, pulling out two small bundles of explosives. Auburn did the same, looking to Kimber to determine where to put them. She pointed haphazardly. She didn't know any more than he did.

"Maybe we can just shoot it," Kim suggested, looking at her railgun before shaking her head. "Nah. Even with how little I know, I suspect that's a really bad idea. What moron would blast a forcefield with that behind it?"

Auburn looked up from the explosives to the blue mass. Kimber was right. Blowing it would be bad.

"Five minutes," Kim said, guessing that would be long enough for them to get back to the airlock and suit up. Outside of that, she had no idea if an explosion in this space would destroy the ship or if there were any other way.

They were both new to space and technology, whether alien or human. "We need to go to school," she said.

"After-action item number forty-seven," Auburn said in his deep, rumbling voice. "Two minutes?"

"How about four, give us time to get back to the airlock." She checked on Petricia's progress. She had Joseph over her shoulder in the fireman's carry. Bundin was working his way into the corridor after her. "Meet you at the airlock."

Auburn placed one pack of explosives by a computer workstation, the type that a human would use.

The ship shuddered and Auburn had to brace himself. Kimber stumbled, but didn't fall. They looked at each other. "What's going on?"

"We are destroying you and your people," the voice chimed in, finally reappearing.

"I doubt that," Kimber replied as she placed a pack of explosives beneath the forcefield containing the swirling blue ball. She stood for a second and then added the second pack to the first.

Auburn slid his second bundle into place beside Kim's. "Just to be sure," he said.

## Alien Ship of the Line #1

"Ted," Terry said softly. "Could we have just blown the explosives we left in those cable bundles?"

Ted looked at Terry through clear eyes as his mind churned. "Yes, I believe that would have stopped the launch."

Terry took a deep breath, his tortured skin protesting the movement. "Why didn't you tell me that instead of trying to kill us all?"

"I can't think of everything. You two are quoting Shakespeare instead of thinking how to fight this thing." Ted waved his hand dismissively, as he was wont to do. He had no idea how much the motion annoyed Terry Henry Walton. Maybe he would have used it more, had he been aware.

"Can you see if the battle's been joined?" Terry asked.

Ted's eyes unfocused as he communed with his AI. "Yes, the fighters from the other carrier launched and have closed on the *War Axe*. They are maneuvering within the heliosphere. All the ships of the blockade are in motion, except this one, the destroyers designated number one and number two, and battleship number two."

"Christina and Joseph," Terry said as he thought aloud.

He moved slowly back to where Cory had stopped working on her mother. Cory's eyes drooped, barely able to stay awake. Char sat up, lucid and looking around.

"Ted tells me we could have accomplished the same thing by blowing the cables in the corridor."

"Now he tells us," Char croaked. "Got a mouthful of whatever that thing was made of."

Char coughed as color slowly returned to her cheeks. Her eyes started to sparkle again.

"Next time, I'll try not to kill us."

"Dying for a cause is noble, TH, but dying because you forgot you put explosives in the wall, unforgiveable. At least no one would have known. What's our next course of action?"

"He's trying to hack the system. We still need the information, but we might be able to help the *War Axe*. If Ted can kill those drones."

Ted's eyes were unfocused and his lips moved slightly as he worked with Plato to fight a battle that no one could see. Ted grimaced, then gritted his teeth. Terry removed his canteen and took a long drink. He handed it to Char, and she finished it. He took out a big chunk of beef jerky and tore it in half. He looked for Dokken, as the dog always appeared with the jerky, but he wasn't there.

"We need to get that dog a suit," Terry said as he handed half of the jerky to Char.

"I get secondhand jerky. Dokken was first?" Char teased before ripping into the meat, providing the fuel her body needed as the nanocytes worked to repair the damage.

Terry refused to look at the back of her head, where some of the hair was still missing. It would grow out in time, but he didn't need to see the stark reminder of his failure to not be ready with a safer course of action.

He shuddered thinking about how close he came to killing them all. He looked to his family, one tear escaping to leave a glistening trail down his cheek.

Cory was asleep with Char holding her, both of them rocking.

"You were born for this moment, to defeat an alien AI on its terms. Get into its head and lay waste, my friend," Terry said softly, trying to encourage the werewolf without interrupting.

*Another mission that has gone completely sideways. Again. FUCK, TH! Get your head out of your ass.*

Terry pinched his face in combined frustration and concentration as he tried to think through other courses of action. He had to fight a space battle against an enemy fleet with one ship. His people had disabled four of the alien heavies. And the *War Axe* had just now become engaged.

She was fighting her own battle. And one man could save them.

That one man wasn't Terry Henry Walton. Maybe it was his ego that needed reassuring. He was out of his element away from Earth, counting on the nanos to fix the damage his people seemed to suffer with increasing frequency.

That was never his intent. He was supposed to stand between the enemy and his command, take the brunt of the damage. Then they'd be free to execute the mission.

The colonel's job was to define the mission in such a way that if they lost communication, every single person would know what it looked like to win. Just in case there was only one survivor, she could finish what they started.

They had lost communication. The Bad Company was killing enemy ships.

Except for Christina and Joseph. What happened to them?

Terry paced as he worked through his personal performance review while waiting for Ted to deliver a miracle. He wanted to know if Christina and Joseph's ships had stopped moving. He wanted to know that the jammer was down so he could talk with the tac teams. He wanted Ted to kill the fighters, because Terry couldn't.

Terry was a grunt, a ground-pounder in a war where all sides were firing plasma weapons. And massive railguns. And missiles.

"I need you to pick up the pace, Ted, and I need you to finish this."

# CHAPTER TWENTY

Ankh tapped away. He'd tuned everything out as the others moved from the area and Christina double-checked the placement of the explosives.

Joseph, Yanmei, and Bundin were long gone. Christina waited.

"Ankh? This mission depends on you. I know you can do it."

He looked up, wearing his usual blank expression. "You said something? I could use a drink and something to eat."

Christina looked down her nose, but he was working, and she wasn't. She removed her canteen and kneeled to hand it to him. She dug a small food bar out of her pack and opened it. When he finished drinking, he took the food bar and folded it to shove the whole thing into his mouth.

While he chewed, he returned to his tablet.

"Ankh? We need to get going. If you could wrap things up, we might be able to get off this tub in one piece."

Ankh ignored her.

Or maybe he hadn't heard. He tapped three more times and ended with a flourish. He looked up at her before turning the pad so she could see. Red lights flashed across a dashboard interface.

"I don't know what I'm looking at," she told him.

"The jamming units have suffered from a cascading failure, and the ship's engines have been disengaged."

"Great news, Ankh!" Christina lightly slapped his small shoulder, before turning her attention to more important matters.

"Bad Company, this is Christina. Ankh has restored communications. Colonel Walton, request status and guidance," Christina said using her backup comm device, the same unit that would remotely activate the explosives.

## Alien Ship of the Line #1

Terry jumped when the comm device buzzed. He pulled it from the shipsuit's breast pocket. The case was slightly melted, but the internals worked.

"Colonel Walton here. Well done, Christina. Well done. Status is, we've stirred up the hornet's nest. Four ships are down, but two of our targets remain active—yours is one, Christina, and the other is Joseph's battleship. Joseph or Kimber, please report."

"Kimber here. Explosives are in place. We have five-minute timers set. Activating now. Joseph is down. An AI called Ten got into his head. His status is unknown."

"Understood," Terry replied, using the Marine Corps comm term for 'I understand.' "If you can dial it to less than five minutes, we'd appreciate that. That battleship is chasing the *War Axe*, I believe."

"Auburn!" Kimber cried.

"I heard. One minute, then?" he said, already changing the first bundle's timer.

"Sounds about right," Kim said softly. They finished changing the timers and ran into the corridor. Kim punched the button and the countdown began.

"Fifty-seven seconds to lights out," Kimber said over the comm device before shoving it in her pocket and focusing her full attention on sprinting through the turning corridors of the alien battleship.

"Ship of the Line Number Two has been stopped. Ankh is still working on the fighters. Do you know their status?"

"Smedley, are you there? Can you answer?" Terry asked.

"Good to hear your voice, Colonel. We are engaged at present, but holding our own. Killing that battleship will be most welcome, but the other ships are trying to hit us with their EMP weapons. We are maintaining our distance through aggressive maneuvers, but our op area is shrinking as they work to box us in. Eliminating the fighters will allow us to focus our firepower on the other ships. Unless you can eliminate them, too, then that would be even more welcome."

"Working on it, General. Tell Dokken that I miss him. Walton out."

"Break, break," Terry said into his device. "By the numbers. Timmons, report."

"Timmons here. Tac Team Werewolf is together and uninjured. We are removing bulkheads at present as we are trying to put some distance between us and the impending explosion that should rip the rear end off this ship." Timmons shook his head, attempting to clear the fog.

Sue knew something was wrong, but he wasn't coming clean. She kept one eye on her mate, in case he went down.

"Sue here. Something is up with Timmons, but he'll be fine once we get off this cursed ship. Give us a few more minutes and we'll be out the airlock."

"Roger," Terry said. "Break, break. Marcie, report."

"Kelly here. We are heading toward the airlock to exfil the tin can, but Marcie is in the mech and on the deck. She's down, and I have no idea why."

Terry looked at Ted. "You need to cut that thing's balls off."

Ted continued his work with Plato. Ted's color was returning, too. His suit was compromised, but it hadn't been shredded like Terry and Char's.

*Why am I in a hurry to leave? Only two of us can get off this ship,* Terry thought. *I'm in a hurry to win, before anyone dies, anyone I know, that is.*

"Keep me informed, Kelly. Break, break. Kaeden, report."

"My team is intact and uninjured. The four of us are trapped in the airlock working to figure out the manual override."

"You'll be protected in there until we can come get you, so don't be in a hurry to get outside."

"I'm not a fan of being trapped in here. We'll get the door open so we can leave. We'll be waiting for pickup. How's the battle going?"

"We are still working to shut down the alien fleet, but right now, the *War Axe* is fighting for her life. All hands, on order, be prepared to take over the ships you are on, secure them as a safehold, until rescue can be arranged."

"Ours is pretty broken," Kae replied softly. "I expect it won't survive the hour."

"Same here," Kelly added.

"And here," Sue reported.

Terry turned in a slow circle, surveying the damage. "I guess we are on borrowed time here, too," he said aloud, before keying the mic on his comm device. "Understood. Do the best you can with what you have, just like you always do. Congratulations, Bad Company. You've accomplished what we set out to do—wreak havoc on the enemy. Now it's up to Ankh and Ted to work their magic, and the *War Axe* to build its cache of battle streamers. Justice has arrived and it looks like us."

Ted looked up. "Give me that," he said, pointing to the comm device. Ted took it from Terry's outstretched hand.

"Ankh, establish a digital link through this device. I have an idea..."

### Alien Ship of the Line #2

Christina handed the device to Ankh. The Crenellian tapped a couple buttons and set it beside his pad. His whole body shook in the strange way that was his race's laugh. He started tapping, his fingers a blur as they raced across the screen.

She wanted to ask what was going on, but Ankh had the comm device. She pursed her lips and turned away. The explosives were in place, but Ankh had the activation unit as part of the comm device. She decided that keeping both close gave her the most options. Even though she was bored, it was time to wait.

She took a seat on the deck next to Ankh, the device within arm's reach. He was embroiled in whatever Ted had him doing and oblivious of her presence.

*How are you two doing?* she asked using her comm chip.

*We have reached the airlock,* Aaron reported.

*Yanmei, get your armor on and stand by. Ankh and Ted are collaborating on something. Once you're inside the suit, you'll have comm with the others. It'll be a little less lonely out there.*

### The *War Axe*

"Helm?" Micky asked.

K'Thrall had been maneuvering the *War Axe* into a tighter and smaller space as he engaged the darting fighters. The alien fleet maneuvered to box him in.

"I need control, Skipper. Our escape window is shrinking."

"Smedley, transfer helm control from COC to Clifton's station."

Micky thought he heard K'Thrall screaming from three decks below.

"Engaging." Helm ran the main engines to the red line, reduced the strain on the attitude thrusters, and made a beeline for the gap between the alien EMP engagement envelopes. The upgrades turned the *War Axe* into the sports car of warships. The starship screamed silently and raced for deep space.

"That's enough. Bring us around to reengage the enemy," Micky said.

The ship continued toward the void.

"I GAVE AN ORDER!" Micky bellowed.

The ship instantly slowed and started a tight turn. "Sorry, I didn't hear. The blood is still pounding in my ears," Clifton replied sheepishly.

"K'Thrall, prepare to reengage. Let's pick them off one by one."

Clifton leaned back. "Moments of sheer terror interspersed by eternities of boredom," he told Dokken. "It's the life of a pilot."

The German Shepherd twisted his head back and forth as he looked at the man. *If you say so.*

"Mac, how are we doing on our shields?" Micky asked, even though he could see the status. They were showing green with minimal damage.

"I think they've modified their weapon. All the damage came from that last attack, where we grazed the EMP envelope. I'm afraid another one or two of those and the shields will be down."

"Very well. Suresha, engine status."

"Engines are green and available at one hundred percent capacity," the commander answered. "Damaged thrusters have been repaired."

Micky knew that they'd come close to overtaxing the engines, but the upgrades had reduced the cooling time. The captain smiled to himself. The *War Axe* had become the ship he'd dreamed of.

"Blagun?"

"No structural issues. Damage control teams remain in place and green."

"Oscar, how are we doing on ammunition?"

"We've expended a great deal already. One more run like that and we'll be out of missiles and almost out of primary railgun projectiles. Secondary load outs are yellow and plasma is green."

"Bracket the enemy using the mains, then turn the ship and we'll attack with a broadside of secondaries as we depart the engagement zone," Micky said, looking at the alien formation's picket ship, the one that they'd chosen to cull from the herd. "Let's go kick some ass."

# CHAPTER TWENTY-ONE

**Alien Ship of the Line #1**

"Woohoo!" Ted hollered before jumping up and starting to dance. Char grinned broadly. Terry smiled too, waiting patiently for Ted's report.

Ted stopped dancing, steeled his expression, and returned to hugging the box that contained Plato, interfacing via his chip.

"What the fuck?" Terry complained.

"We're winning?" Char ventured.

"I suspect, but I'd like to know in what way we're winning."

Cory moaned softly as her eyes slowly opened.

"You're next, Dad," she mumbled.

"No. I'm not. Things are happening so we're hanging on for the ride. You recover to where you can walk. I expect our way ahead will appear shortly."

"What your father is trying to say is we'll do whatever Ted tells us." Char nodded. Terry sighed heavily, turned back to Ted, and waited.

. . .

## Alien Battleship #1

Kim and Auburn sprinted through the corridors, using their enhanced abilities to send them careening ahead, widening the distance between them and the impending explosion. They reached the place where they'd stashed their suits.

Auburn grabbed the hatch activator when the ship rocked and screamed in agony. As one, they pulled their hoods on. The lights went out.

Auburn struggled to remain upright, hanging on tightly to the wheel on the hatch. Kimber fell to her knees, but jumped back up and balanced as if she was surfing. The ship's undulations stopped, and Kim tapped Auburn as she worked her way through the hatch. She found the remaining suit and fumbled into it.

Her enhanced vision wasn't helping since the ship was pitch black inside. Not even the emergency lights were on. The suit's internal systems came to life, bathing her face in a soft electronic glow. She ran through the diagnostics in mere moments, then turned.

"Cover your eyes, lover, I'm hitting the high beams." She gave him a second to look away before activating the suit's lights. She ducked and squeezed through the doorway. Once in the corridor, she headed for the airlock with Auburn close behind.

## The *War Axe*

"The Battleship with Joseph's team on board has experienced a catastrophic explosion in its engine room. The ship is dead and drifting," Smedley reported.

"That's a total of nine ships down. Seven remain along with sixty fighters."

"Fifty-six fighters," Smedley updated. "But the fighter spacecraft are consolidating for a mass attack, instead of the solo hit and run tactics they were using earlier."

"Is that a threat to us?" Micky asked.

"Yes. If they were to employ a suicide attack, they could expedite the demise of the gravitic shields. Their weapons aren't the threat, but their exploding engines would cause significant damage."

"Way to rain on my parade, Smedley. Just when I thought we were doing well, too." Micky stroked his chin as he worked through their current attack plan. Speed was his friend. "Stay the course, K'Thrall."

## Alien Ship of the Line #2

Christina started breathing faster. She didn't like waiting. The strain of doing nothing while a battle raged outside was driving her stress level through the roof. She wanted to change into Pricolici form and tear things apart, just to feel like she was doing something.

But the more she learned about military tactics, the more she embraced finding the enemy's weaknesses, and then exploiting them with the maximum amount of violence at the right time. If that meant waiting, then she would continue to wait.

Even though she hated it.

Ankh tapped away. Every now and then, his small body

would shiver, as if getting ready to go into convulsions, and then he'd go back to what he was doing.

"Ankh, what's the status?" she asked. She couldn't talk with anyone. She couldn't see a map showing the battle. All she could see was the bottom of a terminal, a Crenellian's big head, and a swirling blue mass contained within a forcefield.

"ANKH!" she blurted, before slapping a hand over her mouth.

"Yes?" the small humanoid asked innocently.

"What's the status?"

"We are in the final stage of putting the entity known as Ten behind a separate barrier. It is trying to run, find a way to escape, but Plato is most impressive. We are staying ahead. Standby."

Ankh went back to tapping, rhythmically, followed by a furious dash of fingers, then back to a slower rhythm. This cycle continued for another five minutes. The ship rocked and shuddered twice during that time.

"Ankh. It doesn't feel like you're making progress," Christina said in as soft a tone as she could manage. The ship screeched as if the metal was being twisted. "Ankh? I feel like we should be running away, as fast as we can."

"Hush," Ankh said. Christina's yellow eyes flared for a moment, and she glared at him as her hands itched for the claws needed to shred the Crenellian.

"Okay. We can go now," Ankh said, standing abruptly and bumping his head. He stumbled to one knee, handed Christina the comm device, and wiggled from under the console to stand up anew. He unhooked the wires, letting them lay where they fell, and stuffed his pad into his backpack.

"That's it? What's going on? Is there anything we need to do?" Christina said in a rush. She thumbed the comm device to ask Terry for further instructions when Ankh started to speak.

"We are in control and standing down the alien ships one at a time. They will all be disabled shortly. We have control of the fighters, but we don't. They have a failsafe attack mode. Someone must fly them. And most importantly, we have captured Ten and acquired much of its archives."

Christina breathed a sigh of relief. Her stress dissipated. She looked at the bundles of explosives. The countdown had not begun and wouldn't be needed.

"I can fly a fighter," a voice came over the comm device.

### The *War Axe*

"Give control to Clifton!" Terry Henry's voice resonated through the bridge's comm system. Micky looked at his helm. Clifton shook his head as he tapped at his screen. "Just do it, Ted!"

Clifton nodded as he leaned forward. He brought up the holo screens and took on a new role—squadron commander of the fighters.

The *War Axe* continued to fire. Micky watched as the alien ships' icons changed status from active to inactive. The *War Axe* started to turn away from its attack run, having destroyed a frigate, but two alien destroyers continued to reach out with their EMP weapons.

"Gravitic shields are down," Mac reported.

"Engines are offline," Suresha reported.

Micky's mouth dropped. The ship was racing toward two of the disabled alien vessels.

"Fire all weapons!" Micky shouted.

"Weapons control is offline," K'Thrall said from his console in the COC.

---

Clodagh ran from her workstation into the next space where the manual controls were protected behind a mass of metal and a separately powered shield. She mashed buttons and flipped switches as she tried to establish a manual firing sequence for the thrusters.

The good king Wenceslaus rubbed against her leg, purring.

"I know, I know. Everything will be okay," she muttered as she tried to remember the sequence. She hesitated toward the end. The panel lights were still red.

## Alien Ship of the Line #1

"That's it?" Terry said.

Ted stood up, cradling the black box that contained the AI called Plato. "That was the most intense battle I've ever fought," Ted said, surprised at Terry's lack of gratitude.

"I expect it was," Terry admitted.

Char raised an eyebrow and tipped her head toward Ted. "You are a genius, Ted. Thank you."

"It's about time," Ted replied.

"What about the fighters?" Terry asked.

"Plato, bring up the holo image of the battle."

Nothing happened.

"The projectors must have been damaged in your ill-advised attack upon the ship's engine that almost got us all killed," Ted said accusingly. "Standby."

Terry threw his hands up in frustration, but then started to laugh.

The image flickered to life above their heads. Terry leaned close, studying it. A number of the alien vessels were still green. The *War Axe* remained on a ballistic trajectory into the alien fleet.

"What's going on here?" Terry asked, pointing to the *War Axe*.

Ted communed with Plato for a moment. "The *War Axe* has lost systems control. The EMP weapons overpowered it. It is following the last course before suffering failure."

Terry thumbed his comm device. "Micky, is there anything we can do?"

"Terry! If you could move those two alien tin cans out of the way, we can coast until we can get our systems back online."

Ted shook his head. "Disabling is far easier than enabling. There isn't enough time."

"I'm sorry, Micky," Terry said into his device. He didn't expect an answer.

He didn't get one.

**The *War Axe***

"Brace for impact!" Micky yelled over the ship-wide comm system.

---

Clodagh went back two steps, reversed a switch, and pressed forward. The lights flashed twice and burned green.

"GO!" she yelled at the board. The port-side thrusters activated in unison. Wenceslaus bolted out from under her feet.

His tail was fluffed in a big orange bush and his eyes darted back and forth as he tried to figure out what had scared him.

---

"Thrusters are online," K'Thrall reported. Micky gritted his teeth and winced, expecting an impact with the alien vessel. The *War Axe* lumbered sideways, the thrusters pushing the passing ship away as the *Axe* slid by.

"YES!" Micky shouted, standing. He pulled his hood back and took a deep breath of the bridge's air.

"Helm?" he asked.

Clifton was driving the fighters at the remaining active alien ships. The intense battle was ripping the fighters out of space. Clifton jerked each time one of his ships died.

"Engines, run the forward thrusters until we slow down," Micky ordered over the ship-wide broadcast.

The captain waited, but nothing happened. Helm was

engaged. The ship continued toward deep space at a high rate of speed.

Suddenly, the thrusters kicked in. The ship jerked slightly until antigrav compensated. Micky's board flashed red. "What now?" he said, rolling his head as he looked for the source of his new problem.

"Engines coming back online," Suresha reported. As they cycled through their diagnostics, they flashed red until they passed. It was standard procedure.

"Cargo fleet, this is the *War Axe*. The blockade has ended. Please expedite your transit to Alchon Prime. I expect we have some hungry people over there." Micky sent the message on a narrow beam toward the dots of light beyond the heliosphere.

*Is my human coming home?* Dokken asked.


## Alien Destroyer #2

"Sounds like the battle's over," Kae said into his comm device.

"It is. The *War Axe* will send a drop ship to pick us up. Make sure you can get outside."

"There's the rub," Kae said slowly. "Manual control is jammed. I think we twisted the ship sideways when we blew it up. We are stuck in the airlock."

"I hope you have a deck of cards with you," Terry replied. Kae looked from face to face. His team shook their heads.

"Looking grim on that front."

"Don't worry. I won't tell anyone," Terry said, broadcasting to anyone with a comm device.

"I printed some pages from this cool game they played when you were growing up. Role-playing mutants and humans on a massive colony ship. We'll game a bit to pass the time," Kae said.

"Sounds like Metamorphosis Alpha," Terry said fondly.

"It is," his son replied.

"It won't seem like you're waiting. Enjoy the theater of the mind, Kaeden. We will be there as soon as practicable to pick you up. We'll bring torches."

Kaeden dug in his backpack with his armored hand. He pulled out a small sheaf of papers and started to read out loud. They kept their hoods in place within the partially depressurized airlock.

"We don't have any dice," Cap said.

"We'll make do."

"My character is going to die, isn't he?"

"Probably…"

Kae's comm device crackled. "When you come to pick us up, bring extra shipsuits. Ours are in pretty bad shape, and I don't think we're the only ones," Terry's voice proclaimed.

# CHAPTER TWENTY-TWO

"Seventeen hours, total, for the infiltration operation," Smedley told the group gathered around the conference table.

The chairs had been removed and that solved the space problem for the small army that Terry kept bringing to the meetings.

Nathan Lowell watched them from the screen on the wall. He nodded slowly. He had thought it would take it a week.

"Cargo ships?" Terry asked, tipping his beer back for a long drink. It was his new ritual. Finish a mission, have a beer. A successful mission, have two. His second sat on the table, waiting for him to finish his first. Terry's free hand was on Dokken's head, absently scratching behind the German Shepherd's ears. Char joined TH in keeping a hand wrapped up in the dog's fur.

"First deliveries have already been made. The ships are stacked and offloading as quickly as they can. They'll requeue to load up with outbound cargo, but for now, they are on the road to recovery."

"Losses?" Terry wondered.

Micky looked down. "Alien fleet took out two ships before we arrived. They were never able to restore power. Those two crews are gone. One hundred and seventy five died on the planet during the blockade."

"We lost a couple hundred people," Terry whispered, grimacing at the thought.

"Marcie, what's the capture count?" Terry knew the number. He didn't forget things like that.

"We have one fully intact Ship of the Line, hat tip to Christina, with eighty fighters, twenty that survived the battle and all the ones trapped on the other carrier," she reported, nodding to her parents. "We have one battleship, four destroyers, and four frigates. The remaining fleet is space junk after K'Thrall conducted a little extra target practice with the mains. We've deployed warning buoys around the area. We have nearly a thousand prisoners that we've consolidated on the alien carrier that we're calling Sheri's Pride."

"Sheri's Pride?" Micky asked.

"The wife of one of our squad leaders. She's like the den mother, teaching the warriors social skills and stuff like that. Some of us would rather be in combat than study which fork is right for which course. We thought naming it after her might make her go easier on us. And, all the captives are male. We figured putting them on a ship named after a woman would be an eye-opening experience, along with breaking them in on the reality of equality." Marcie smiled in Christina's direction, acknowledging that the idea was hers.

Kae had ordered six mechs to the ship and Kimber had put the remainder of her platoon over there to keep the peace. Fitzroy was in charge with Capples acting as his executive.

"The prisoners aren't giving us any trouble. Theirs is to obey," Kimber added. "I think they like being free of the mental games and interacting with other humans who are genuinely interested in their well-being. Plus, they are keeping the ship in tip-top condition. Plato is running things from an AI standpoint, there, and on all the captured ships."

"What's the status of the entity known as Ten?" Nathan interjected. He had read the status in the report, but wanted to hear it firsthand.

Ted pointed to the black box on the table. "Plato and Ten have traded places. External links from within the box have been physically removed. All that Ten is exists within this space." Ted drew a box with his hands around the black box. Ankh's oversized Crenellian head squeezed into place beside Ted and peered over the edge of the table. Ankh nodded knowingly.

"How can we study it?" Nathan wondered, squinting to better see the table and the mystery on it.

"Ten is extremely dangerous," Ted said, tipping his chin up to look down at the people in the room. "It took a great deal of effort to bring it down. Opening Ten up to the outside world will be a challenge. I recommend that Ten be transferred to R2D2 under maximum security for study.

Don't be confused. This is an alien entity that acts like an AI."

Nathan pursed his lips and whistled. "Can we launch it into the sun?" he asked, knowing that he would not accept that course of action.

"There is more of Ten. The place that the human cattle called Home World. Killing this one won't end that threat. We need to continue the interrogation until we know all that Ten knows," Ted explained more patiently than usual.

"What about the EMP weapon. Who did Ten get that from?" Nathan said, leaning forward until his face filled the screen.

"I have no idea who Ten got it from, but we stole it from the entity," Ted replied. Nathan looked confused. Ted didn't elaborate.

"How did we take it from the entity?"

"A dead ship that R&D bought from some scavenger. It had Ten's EMP technology. Turns out that ship was a deep space probe. Which suffered a catastrophic failure because the human labor that Ten nurtured and trained wasn't very good. We reverse-engineered the weapon from there, but that little tidbit never made it into the official database."

Nathan chuckled. "A genius discovery that was based on luck."

"Isn't that where most breakthroughs come from?" Terry asked. Ted looked at Terry as if he was stupid. "Just asking a question, that's all. Ninety-nine percent perspiration and one percent inspiration, that kind of thing."

Ted didn't dignify it with a reply.

"When are we going to Ten's so-called Home World?"

Char said, her voice cold and face set. Terry nodded and took another drink.

"We have a population to liberate," Terry said.

"Bring up the galaxy map, please," Nathan requested.

Micky talked softly with Smedley and the galaxy appeared.

"Zoom in on Alchon Prime, and also show Keeg Station. Now add where we think Home World is. And finally, put in Benitus Seven."

Alchon Prime stood within the extensive Federation belt that bordered the frontier. Keeg Station was off the beaten path, but within Federation space. Home World was well outside the Federation and Benitus Seven was in between, on the edge of the known frontier.

"Talk to us about Benitus Seven, Nathan. How do you even contact someone that far out?" Terry leaned forward as he tried to guess the distances.

"Benitus Seven is a planet of non-humanoids. They naturally commune with the Etheric, so we've been able to contact them in that dimension. No human has been to their planet, not as far as we know, anyway. There is a growing concern regarding a tear in the interdimensional boundary."

Terry made a strange face. "Sounds like a job for scientists. Why would the Direct Action Branch be involved with something like that?"

"There are some baddies coming through and they seem to have a singular goal of removing all life on Benitus Seven. They only have a small foothold now and the Benitons have been able to put some roadblocks in their way, but they need help. Before the month's out, I need you there to resolve the situation by eliminating this enemy."

"Are you picking our target for us, Nathan?" Terry asked. He had other missions on the front burner because they'd prioritized the missions based on the RFPs, the requests for proposals.

"In this case, I am. It is a directed mission. The payment is nothing less than miniaturized Etheric power sources for our ships. You want gate technology on your drop ships? This is what it will take."

"A drop ship that could gate in?" Terry exclaimed.

"Can I get a sample to study now?" Ted asked.

"They are on Benitus Seven," Nathan replied.

"What are we waiting for?" Ted wondered, glaring at Terry.

"Don't you want to see Felicity? Tell her all the evil things I did to you?"

Ted looked defiant. "Damn right!" Char raised one eyebrow and started to chuckle.

"Damn straight. We're going back to Keeg Station for repairs, transfer Ten to a max security safe hold, drop off the captives and our booty." Terry smiled. He never wanted to be a pirate, except when he always wanted to be a pirate. That was why he had taken up sailing in the first place. "We've added a few ships to our fleet, Nathan, and we need to get them reconfigured into a proper combat force. We'll start that process, with Felicity's help and a thousand new dock workers, and then we'll go to Benitus Seven on our way to Home World."

"I'll forward the Benitus mission brief to your private

channel. Just so you're ready, here's an image of one of the invaders."

The three-dimensional galaxy faded, replaced by the picture of a creature with red, fibrous skin, pointed ears, and horns.

"Looks like the devil," Terry stated matter-of-factly as he chewed on the inside of his cheek.

"That's right," Nathan replied. "The stories about the devil weren't fantasy or horror. These creatures exist on the other side of the Etheric, and now they've found their way onto Benitus."

### The End of Blockade, Book 2 of The Bad Company

*If you like this book, please leave a review. I have to partition my time and with a number of series needing attention, I will give the next story to the one with the most reviews. It could be The Bad Company. That depends on you, the readers.*

*Please, help me to best prioritize.*

*Don't stop now! Keep turning the pages as Craig & Michael talk about their thoughts on this book and the overall project called the Age of Expansion (and if you haven't read the ten-book prequel, the Terry Henry Walton Chronicles, now is a great time to take a look).*

*Terry, Char, and the rest of the Bad Company's Direct Action Branch will return in Price of Freedom.*

## AUTHOR NOTES - CRAIG MARTELLE
### DECEMBER 15, 2017

Thank you for reading beyond the end of the book and all the way to the author notes. You are the bomb!

And Merry Christmas! Happy Hanukkah, Happy Festivus, Happy RamaHanuKwanzMas, or simply, Happy Monday. I want everyone to be happy all the time and although that isn't possible, I can still want it.

If you join my mailing list (stop by www.craigmartelle.com and look for the sign up link), you'll get notified on release day for every new book in this series, and **every new book is only 99 cents on the Saturday of release week**, as a reward for those who are on my newsletter list and follow me on Facebook. Thank you very much for coming on board. There are so many stories left to tell.

And I still live in the Sub-Arctic.

It's that time of year where it is hard to tell what time of day it is. It's dark most of the time. It's cold, not really cold, but temps have only gotten down to minus twenty or so a few times. Nothing too extreme. They are hovering around zero Fahrenheit which is about normal. Average temperature in January is minus ten. We'll see if it drops to hit the average.

We had a lot of snow before it got cold, so the picnic table is completely buried. The tractor is working magnificently, and I have already moved a veritable mountain of snow this winter.

I got the flu when I went to Las Vegas and it lingered for an obscene amount of time, despite taking a great deal of time off. I watched three full seasons of Babylon 5 and have started the fourth season. All the while, doing nothing but watching and napping. That still didn't help. Do you know what finally helped me kick it? A weeklong trip to Hawaii. The heat and sea air helped me over the final hump on the road to recovery. Thank goodness. I have way too much to do to not work for weeks at a time.

I needed some more character names so I canvassed my friends and fans and here's what we have. Sheri is in honor of Sheri Mellott's 29th birthday. She and Frank are good friends from well before I started writing. Finally, she makes it into one of my books. Happy Birthday, Sheri!

The dive restaurant, Click, Click, Boom (the activation sequence on a claymore mine) and the author within is a shout out to my friends and fellow authors, Jonathan Yanez and Justin Sloan for their book of the same title set within Justin's Seppukarian universe.

I am managing the Age of Expansion area for the Kurtherian Gambit Universe (Michael Anderle's fabulous creation). We had a great launch of a few new books, the successor series following Gateway to the Universe. The Ghost Squadron by Sarah Noffke and JN Chaney has been well received. Thank you to the kind readers for embracing that story line.

A number of people helped me with some language. I want to thank Robert Tonkiss for his "nose in a snit" comment because I was lamenting the fact that The Bad Company had received a few two-star reviews. But the Bad Company was a deviation from what people were used to with the Terry Henry Walton Chronicles and despite the fact that we used Gateway to the Universe as a transition book, some people still didn't like the shift, or as Robert said, they got their nose in a snit. I'm sorry that some readers didn't take the new book as well as I would have liked, but I was done with the Nomad story line as it was. I simply cannot churn out more of the same. I enjoy the new lives and new challenges that await Terry and Char as they help expand the Federation.

That's it – break's over, back to writing the next book. Peace, fellow humans.

---

Please join my Newsletter (www.craigmartelle.com – please, please, please sign up!), or you can follow me on Facebook since you'll get the same opportunity to pick up the books for only 99 cents on that first day they are published.

**If you liked this story, you might like some of my other books.** You can join my mailing list by dropping by my website **www.craigmartelle.com** or if you have any comments, shoot me a note at craig@craigmartelle.com. I am always happy to hear from people who've read my work. I try to answer every email I receive.

If you liked the story, please write a short review for me on Amazon. I greatly appreciate any kind words, even one or two sentences go a long way. The number of reviews an ebook receives greatly improves how well an ebook does on Amazon.

Amazon – www.amazon.com/author/craigmartelle

Facebook – www.facebook.com/authorcraigmartelle

My web page – www.craigmartelle.com

Twitter – www.twitter.com/rick_banik

Well, now that Lord of the Cosmos (LotC) Craig has co-opted my "Thank you for reading the story and NOW, reading the author notes as well" comment, I guess I have to go back and rely on an old and dependable start.

HELLO!

(Didn't see that one coming, did you? You did? Well...*shit*.)

TKG is over two years old, and now the 'official' full expansion of going with collaborators just turned 1 years old on December 8th. In this year, we have stretched and expanded with new ages, new series, wonderful collaborators and a bump in the road (or two.)

**How do all of these stories fit together?**

To answer that questions, I usually send fans to the websites and the timeline(s). One of them seeks to place the answers into a real timeline, but is behind on the updates. The other is more up to date on the books, but isn't quite as pretty.

The second timeline (Clickable) is here: http://kurtherianbooks.com/timeline-kurtherian/

The first timeline (Printable) is here: http://kurtherianbooks.com/timeline-kurtherian-printable/

We are JUST getting started with the Age of Expansion here at the end of 2017, and have many other series planned or in the very early stage. We even have one series with a new author where I would describe the series as a cross between Boston Legal and maybe a Judge Dredd? We are still working on it at the moment.

**DO YOU LIKE AUDIO? Or do you *LOVE* audio?**

On another front, we have well over fifty audiobooks published, and will be doing MORE this year. I imagine we will continue our effort of five to six books a month for the foreseeable future. If you have a particular series which you would like to hear on Audible that we don't have yet, drop a line to Stephen Campbell at Readershelp@Kurtherianbooks.com and give him a shout to put the request in the queue!

*How do you find out about new books to listen to?*

Also, if you like audio can you let us know HOW you find out about new audiobooks? (Send to the same email as above – *Readershelp*.) We are struggling with our marketing in this audio arena. Further, we would love to know how you hear about, see, click on adverts, or whatever way you learn about books that are on audio and how you choose to use your credits, or purchase the books.

**German Editions**

I like to speak to some things that LMBPN Publishing has accomplished from time to time that I find cool, without sounding like a total shill for us because I'm excited with what we have done. It is beyond me that two years ago, I had just released my fourth book and I am just now seeing a $100 day of sales and thinking "Can I maybe do this as a living?"

This time, I'm going to say WHOOP because Death Becomes Her has been published in German (the language) and is titled Mutter der Nacht. The reason we can't use Death Becomes Her is German law about duplicating titles in the country.

Thanks to a crack team (I'll speak about them more, later) we have Queen Bitch heading to German release at end the of January.

Thank you SO MUCH for coming on this adventure with us, we can't do what we do without you.

Ad Aeternitatem,
Michael Anderle

adventure

Mystically Engineered (co-written with Valerie Emerson) – dragons in space

Monster Case Files (co-written with Kathryn Hearst) – a young-adult cozy mystery series

*For a complete list of books from Craig, please see www. craigmartelle.com*

Made in the USA
Las Vegas, NV
03 October 2022